Prologue

In ancient times, there existed an oracle named Eamon Pompeanus. Eamon was believed to possess eyes that could see energy, enabling the creation of powerful techniques. The Oracle was said to have had two sons. The eldest son led the Pompeanus Clan, inheriting the power of the Oracle's eyes, while the other son inherited the Oracle's power to manipulate energy. The Pompeanus Clan, led by the descendants of the first son, continued in their sacred duty to amass wealth and power, while the descendants of the other son went on to establish the Knights of Rome, an order dedicated to defending Rome and fostering peace. These Knights were believed to have wielded immense powers, including telekinesis, regeneration, mind reading, and telepathy.

By the year 2000 AD, the Knights of Rome had been extinct for centuries. This has led many to doubt their existence, as few historical records remain. Back then, the Pompeanus Clan had access to an empty dimension known as the Pompeanus Dimension. However, no Pompeani has entered the dimension for years, leading many to doubt its existence and that of their founder, Eamon Pompeanus.

Currently, the world is divided among several major nations: The Roman Republic, The Norse Kingdom, and The Yuan Empire.

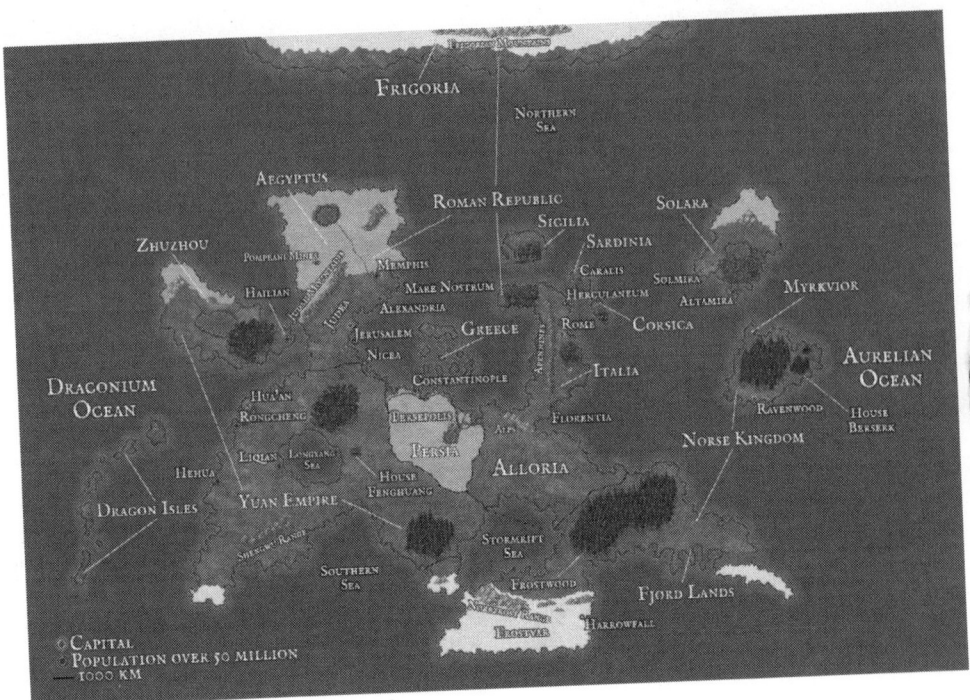

The Roman Republic is at war with the Yuan Empire, a conflict that has lasted for decades, with neither side making any significant territorial gains. A twenty-kilometer wide zone separates these two nations.

Faunus Virelius, a descendant of the Pompeanus Clan, awakens powers thought to have been lost for centuries. An ancient prophecy from the Oracle of Pompeani marks him and another with intertwining destinies. Alongside his family and friends, Faunus must confront oppressive forces seeking to destroy the legacy of the Knights of Rome and any remaining semblance of freedom.

Table of Contents

Prologue....1

Chapter One....4

Chapter Two....13

Chapter Three....19

Chapter Four....26

Chapter Five....46

Chapter Six....73

Chapter Seven....85

Chapter Eight....96

Chapter Nine....111

Chapter Ten....122

Chapter Eleven....135

Index....145

Chapter One

The Prophecy

In deep space, there lay an asteroid, nestled within the asteroid belt between Mars and Jupiter. This asteroid, known as Astra Eamon, was not like the others; it was a sanctuary amidst the barren void.

Atop Astra Eamon, a magnificent glass dome stood. The dome, crafted by ancient Pompeani, shimmered in the sunlight. Within this dome, a lush garden thrived as verdant vines draped over the stone archways and flowers of every hue bloomed. Trees with leaves like emerald fire reached towards the heavens, their branches cradling the stars.

In the heart of this garden, seated upon a throne of intertwined roots and vines, was the Pompeani Oracle. His ancient visage was weathered, and he had a long white beard.

As the sun, a distant golden orb, cast its light through the dome, it bathed the Oracle's face in a cascade of warmth. The light refracted through the dome, painting the garden in hues of gold.

Suddenly, the Oracle's eyes were revealed. He possessed the Spectoculo, an eye that allows the user to see and manipulate energy.

It was then that two comets, blazing with tails of bright white fire, crossed each other's paths in the sky. The garden seemed to hold its breath as the celestial bodies traced a sigil in the stars.

The Oracle spoke, "When two comets cross the sky, two eyes will appear. One eye against the other. The fate of the world rests on the result of their battle. The eyes of old will determine the course of the future."

Meanwhile, back on earth, a 16 year old boy named Faunus Virelius darted through a crowded street in the heart of Rome.

Faunus, a descendant of the ancient Pompeani clan, had a mischievous glint in his eyes.

His brown hair fluttered as he ran, and he wore a black jacket with the Pompeani Crest, an illustration of the sun. A white tunic peeked out from underneath.

His teacher ran after him and shouted, "Faunus! Faunus, come back!" Panting, she wondered aloud, "How's he so fast?"

Faunus continued running with ease. He laughed, "Good luck catching me this time! I'm finally going to see it, the Knights of Rome's Castle!"

As she caught her breath, the museum curator approached her and asked, "What's all the commotion?"

The teacher explained, "One of my students ran off towards the castle."

His expression became serious. "That area is off limits," he said. "The government doesn't want anyone within a kilometer of the wall unless you live there, but even then, you are forbidden from approaching the castle."

Meanwhile, Faunus reached a massive steel wall at the end of the street. He thought, "I wonder what they don't want people to see." He started to climb the ledges of a nearby building, but three stories up, he missed a ledge and began to fall.

As he was falling, he said to himself, "This is it, I'm going to die without ever seeing it." Suddenly, he found himself in an empty, white void. He shouted, "Hello!" but there was no response.

The Pompeani Oracle appeared before him and said, "Child of Pompeani, you have awakened the Optoculo, the eye possessed by our ancestor, Eamon Pompeanus. With this eye, you shall usher in a new era. However, beware that another possesses the same eye. The eye that unlocks its full potential will be victorious. The eye that is victorious will determine the fate of this world."

Suddenly, the Oracle vanished as Faunus lay in the street. He stood up, wondering if it was a dream, but once he looked at his reflection in a window, he noticed his right eye had changed. His eye now appeared blue with a white swirl pattern.

He heard voices calling his name, so he quickly climbed back up the building, this time with ease. Once he reached the top, he was in awe at the sight.

The Knights of Rome's Castle, situated on a hill, had cracked stone steps leading up to the outer stone wall, with an archway above the entrance. The castle stood several stories tall and had a lower level surrounded by marble pillars with a slanted red tile roof. On top, a narrower upper level was situated.

He wondered, "How do I get down?"

Faunus looked down and closed his eyes before stepping off the ledge. He instinctually extended his hand, slowing his dissent as he landed.

Faunus, looking up, thought, "How did I do that?"

He turned and walked up the steps leading into the castle. Once inside, he looked around the courtyard, observing ancient statues. He continued into the atrium, where he saw a sword with an inscription that read, "This sword once belonged to Mark Anthony."

As he continued exploring, he heard a sound. He cautiously made his way back to the main atrium, dimly lit by the light pouring in from the wall outlets.

He heard a voice, "My master foretold you would be here. I've been waiting a long time for you."

A figure then leapt down and approached him. Faunus could see that he was around his age and possessed the same eye he had but in his left eye. His other eye resembled the Oracle's. Faunus, curious, asked, "Are you the Oracle?"

He introduced himself, "I'm Silvius." Without any warning, Silvius released an energy blast that sent Faunus flying into a wall.

Faunus, determined, got back on his feet. His right eye was pulsing, and he could feel energy coursing through his body. He then extended his hand towards Silvius, releasing a blast of energy, launching him into a wall.

Silvius' gaze drifted into the distance as he recalled a painful memory. He found himself in the dimly lit training hall in Lord Vespasian's compound. The voice of Lord Vespasian echoed, "You're weak, Silvius. I shouldn't even bother with you," as he kicked him.

Silvius, gritting his teeth, said, "I'm trying to awaken my eye."

Lord Vespasian glared as he unleashed lightning from his fingertips, eliciting a scream of agony from Silvius. He said, "Your eye still hasn't reached its full potential. If you fail me, you'll be severely punished."

The memory faded, pulling Silvius back to the present. He found himself amidst a pile of rubble as Faunus stood in the center of the room.

Suddenly, the Oracle appeared. "The time for your fight has not yet come," he said.

Silvius' eye then pulsed as he vanished. Faunus, terrified, stammered, "How did you get here? Where did he go?"

The Oracle, with a serene expression, replied, "I'm using the last of my strength to project myself to you with an ability created by a Knight long ago. As for Silvius, I activated his eye and sent him to the Pompeanus Dimension. He'll manage to return shortly, so I recommend you leave immediately."

Without a second thought, Faunus sprinted out of the castle. As he reached the top of the wall, he looked back towards the castle before turning around to face the city. He then leapt down into the street below.

Meanwhile, his classmates were lining up outside the museum. Faunus snuck into the line, brushing his hair over his right eye to conceal it.

His teacher, seeing him, exclaimed, "Faunus! You caused a lot of problems today! Where were you?"

Faunus, breathing heavily, replied, "I got lost on my way to see the castle. I'm sorry."

The teacher, relieved, said, "I'm glad you're alright but your mom will be hearing about this!"
As Faunus stood in line, he thought about what had happened. He then boarded the hover transport and looked back towards the steel wall surrounding the castle.

Once the transport arrived at Caralis, Faunus met up with his friends.

Caralis had numerous skyscrapers arranged in tiers, starting from the beach that overlooks the deep blue waters of the Mediterranean. As the city ascended from the coast, the tiers continued upward, culminating in the Financial District and the Forum at the top. Following the destruction of Corsica, the remaining Pompeani established a thriving community in Caralis' Financial District, where Faunus' house is located.

Lucius, one of Faunus' friends, was 15 years old with dark hair and brown eyes. He wore a red tunic. Marcus, his other friend, was 16 years old with orange curly hair and green eyes. He wore a white tunic. Aelia, also 16, had long, straight brown hair and blue eyes. She wore a white skirt with an embroidered pattern around the waist.

"You won't believe what happened today!" Faunus exclaimed as he recounted his day.

"Did you really see the Knight's Castle?" Lucius asked.

"And what's this about a special eye?" Marcus chimed in, leaning closer.

Faunus replied, "I did. As for my eye, I'm not sure what it does yet."

"Do I look any different to you?" Aelia asked, her face slightly red.

Faunus replied, "No, you look the same as always."

Aelia asked, "So, do I usually look good then?"

Faunus looked at her and replied, "Today you do."

Aelia, annoyed, shouted, "Faunus, you're always so rude!"

Faunus replied, "Okay… Okay… you look good all the time."

Aelia turned her head away and said, "No, you don't actually think that."

Faunus put his arm around her and said, "You know you're cute, Aelia; you don't need me to tell you that."

Aelia turned away as she blushed.

Marcus said, "Faunus, you made her blush."

Lucius followed up, "She's in love with you, Faunus."

Aelia angrily replied, "I am not!"

Faunus laughed, "I tend to have that effect on people."

Faunus' mother appeared at the door, her arms crossed with a frown on her face. Faunus, seeing her, quickly waved goodbye to his friends.

"Hi, Mom… Our field trip went well…" Faunus began, but before he could finish, his mother pinched his ear.

She scolded, "Your teacher called me earlier. Do you know what would've happened if a government official caught you?"

"But Mom, Uncle Ireneus works for Cohort 13, and he used to command an entire legion. I'd be fine," Faunus tried to reason.

His mother's voice rose, "You know what happened to your father when he tried to go against the government! Your Uncle couldn't help him when he disappeared. Promise me, you'll never do something that reckless again!"

"I promise! I promise! Please let me go," Faunus pleaded.

Later that night, Faunus' uncle came home. Uncle Ireneus was an older man with gray hair and a long beard. He is slightly stout, and he wore a red tunic.

He found Faunus on the balcony, looking up at the stars. "Not much of a view, unfortunately," Ireneus said with a smile.

He said, "I heard what happened. Your mother is just trying to protect you, as am I. So, how was the castle?"

Faunus' eyes widened. "How did you...? I didn't see it?"

Ireneus laughed, "I know you did. You've been wanting to see it for years."

"It was incredible, Uncle. It's almost like I could feel their presence," Faunus exclaimed.

"That makes sense. Your ancestors were Knights, but that's only half your ancestry; your other ancestors are descended from the Pompeanus Clan," Ireneus replied.

Faunus said, "So that's why I have the eye."

"What eye?" Ireneus asked.

Before Faunus could answer, his mother called them to dinner. They gathered around the table and gave thanks for their food. Ireneus spoke about current issues in Cohort 13 and the war with the Yuan Empire. When he mentioned Pompeani and the Knights of Rome, Faunus' mother scolded him for encouraging Faunus' curiosity.

After dinner, Faunus and Aelia went for a walk. They continued through the streets until they reached an observation deck overlooking the sea.

Aelia said, "This place is beautiful, Faunus."

Faunus replied, "I like coming here."

Suddenly, they heard an air siren. A voice announced over the loudspeakers, "All citizens, take cover immediately."

As they heard explosions in the distance, Aelia lost her footing and slipped off the ledge. Faunus, with adrenaline surging, extended his hand, freezing her in midair. He slowly raised his hand, safely moving her back onto the ledge.

Aelia was too astonished to speak. Faunus shouted, "Get behind me!" as a bomb exploded in front of them. His eye then activated, transporting them to the Pompeanus Dimension.

Shortly afterward, Faunus and Aelia returned. Aelia lay unconscious, overwhelmed by shock. Faunus began to look around, viewing the destruction. Soon after, an announcement blared over the loudspeakers, "All enemy aircraft have been destroyed. Damage control teams have been dispatched to all affected areas."

Faunus carried Aelia back to her house before returning home. His mother greeted him at the door, tears streaming down her face, as she hugged him tightly.

Later that night, Uncle Ireneus came into his room. "Faunus, I see that your clothes are scorched, so you must have been near an explosion, but you seem to be alright. Also, I only caught a glimpse of your eye, but what I saw appeared to be the Spectoculo," Ireneus said.

Faunus brushed his hair aside, revealing his right eye. "This is the Optoculo, but it looks similar to the Spectoculo," Faunus explained.

Uncle Ireneus was speechless for a moment. Faunus continued, "This eye allows me to wield strange powers but sometimes it acts on its own." He demonstrated by lifting a book from across the room.

Uncle Ireneus smiled and said, "You too." He then stretched out his hand and lifted the book above Faunus' head.

Chapter Two

The Optoculo

Uncle Ireneus watched as Faunus strained to lift a heavy stone. The training area behind the house had a large boulder beside a pond teeming with colorful fish. Their movements created ripples that lapped against the smooth pebbles lining the water's edge. Lush green grass stretched out beneath their feet.

"You see, Faunus," Uncle Iren began, "The Optoculo likely allows you to manipulate energy similar to how the Knights once did. It's also possible that you've inherited this ability from your father and I."

Faunus listened intently as he focused on the stone. Sweat trickled down his forehead as his muscles tensed.

"Picture yourself lifting the object," Uncle Ireneus instructed calmly. "Feel its weight. Imagine it rising into the air."

Faunus closed his eyes as the stone began to levitate.

Later that evening, Faunus and Aelia sat across from each other in a restaurant.

Aelia said, "Thank you for saving me, Faunus."

Faunus replied, "No problem." He sighed, "I've been training all day, but I still haven't been able to use my eye."

Aelia responded, "But you used it the other night."

Faunus admitted, "That's the only time."

Aelia smiled as she took out her contacts, revealing the Spectoculo.

Faunus, astonished, asked, "Since when?"

Aelia laughed, "I've always had it, silly. My parents asked me to keep it a secret since Pompeani with it have gone missing."

She suggested, "What if we go to Mars? The Pompeani there may know more about your eye."

That night, Faunus approached his uncle with the plan.

Ireneus thought for a moment and said, "We better get ready to leave."

Faunus exclaimed, "Thank you, Uncle!"

The next morning, they boarded Ireneus' shuttle. As it lifted off, Faunus pressed his face against the window as Caralis disappeared.

Faunus said, "I've never been to space before."

Aelia replied, "I've only been once with my family, and that was ages ago."

Faunus turned to Ireneus and asked, "How many planets have you been to?"

Ireneus replied, "I've traveled across the solar system and seen many planets."

Faunus asked, "What is that?" as they passed through a massive metal ring.

Ireneus explained, "The entrance to a space lane."

Aelia asked, "What's a space lane?"

Ireneus replied, "Space lanes are corridors clear of debris so ships can travel safely." He then paid the toll and activated the coaxial drive, arriving at Mars within minutes.

The shuttle soon landed in Eamon City, a cluster of interconnected domes made of glass. Inside these domes, skyscrapers reached towards the sky as lush gardens grew below. High speed trains ran throughout the city, connecting the different areas. They then boarded the hover train.

Faunus turned to Aelia and said, "This city is so cool!"

Aelia replied, "I can't wait to see the Cultural Center, and learn more about your eye."

Faunus responded, "Me too."

After arriving at the Pompeani Cultural Center, they walked through a hall with a marble floor and a gold ceiling. They continued on until they reached the archives, where they were greeted by Felix.

Uncle Ireneus said, "A brother seeks refuge here."

Felix asked, "Who are they?"

Ireneus answered, "Those who have tasted the fruit of wisdom."

Felix smiled and said, "Welcome, General Ireneus. We're honored to have a Grandmaster visit. If you would follow me."

Faunus whispered to Uncle Iren, "What was that about?"

Uncle Ireneus smiled, "He's just an old friend."

Akari and Berserk greeted them.

"I didn't expect to see you here, Ireneus." Berserk said.

"We have some questions about an eye," Uncle Iren replied.

Akari glanced at Aelia and said, "Yes, the girl possesses the Spectoculo. It grants sensory abilities and, in some cases, allows the user to see and manipulate energy."

Faunus stepped forward, revealing his Optoculo.

"The Optoculo," Berserk said.

"You know about my eye?" Faunus asked eagerly.

Berserk instructed, "Yes, all of you, follow me."

They descended into the ancient underground archives. Berserk deactivated an energy barrier as he retrieved an ancient, worn scroll.

"This scroll was written by Eamon Pompeanus, the founder of the Pompeanus Clan. I'll translate,"

"*As my final days approach, I look back on my life with regret and hope for the future. My firstborn son has led our clan down a path that will only lead to destruction. I am hopeful that future generations may awaken my eyes and lead our clan on a better path. The Optoculo, which allows the user to visualize energy and enter an empty dimension, is the transitional stage to awakening the Transoculo, which allows the user to effortlessly move through space. Possessing the Transoculo in both eyes enhances the user's ability. I came to possess these eyes as a result...*"

The scroll ended abruptly.

Berserk explained, "Some believe that the eyes awakened by Eamon Pompeanus were the result of a random mutation, while others believe it was a gift from God. There's an ancient prophecy that the one who awakens the Optoculo," but he was interrupted by Faunus.

"I already know the prophecy," Faunus said. "The Oracle told me."

Berserk, surprised, asked, "You spoke with the Oracle?"

Faunus, nodding his head, replied, "Yes, he was... strange."

Berserk shouted, "The Pompeani Oracle is wise! You should show him more respect."

Faunus laughed nervously, "Sorry." He added, "I also fought someone who possessed the Optoculo."

Aelia smacked him on the head. "Why didn't you mention this earlier?"

Berserk sighed, "He must be the other mentioned in the prophecy."

Uncle Iren asked, "What's his name?"

"Silvius," Faunus replied. "He had the Optoculo in his left eye and a Spectoculo in the other."

Berserk responded, "That's problematic. With that second eye, he could be more powerful than you."

"We must begin your training immediately," Uncle Iren insisted.

Over the next few days, Faunus trained diligently, learning more about Pompeanus Clan and the Optoculo.

One evening, Uncle Ireneus instructed, "I want you to focus, Faunus. Close your eyes and sense the energy around you."

Faunus asked, "What now?"

Uncle Iren replied, "I want you to focus on something." He asked, "What are you focusing on?"

Faunus replied, "Aelia."

Uncle Ireneus asked, "Where is she?"

Faunus answered, "She's by you, uncle."

He then put his hands together, continuing to concentrate.

Faunus wondered aloud, "I wonder if I can sense my mom from here."

Uncle Iren warned, "Sensing someone far away requires much more energy. That energy can be felt by certain individuals, like myself, and Silvius."

Faunus, ignoring his uncle's warning, focused intently on his mom.

Uncle Ireneus said to himself, "He's taking in the energy around him," as Faunus began to glow white.

His right eye then began to pulse as an enormous amount of energy emanated from him.
Lord Vespasian, sensing Faunus, said, "So, he's the one."

Meanwhile, in a dark prison in the Yuan Empire, a man sat up in his cell and said, "My son."

Chapter Three

The Return of Decimus

As Faunus awoke, he looked up to see Aelia and his uncle sitting by him.

Uncle Ireneus asked, "You okay, Faunus?"

Faunus, putting his hand over his eye, replied, "I think I'm alright."

Aelia said, "Thank goodness, that's a relief."

Uncle Ireneus said, "After you opened your right eye, you began to take in energy. Your sensory powers also became extremely potent. However, your technique was imperfect, causing you to take in too much energy." He sighed, "Everyone in the solar system probably sensed you."

Faunus looked down in disappointment.

Uncle Iren turned to Berserk and said, "We have to go."

Berserk locked wrists with him and replied, "Thank you for coming." He turned to Faunus and said, "Faunus, keep up with your training."

Faunus replied, "I will."

They then boarded the hover train and departed the Cultural Center.

Meanwhile, in a prison in the Yuan Empire, Decimus plotted his escape.

The facility was surrounded by an impenetrable energy shield and three fortified walls. The only entrance was a reinforced gate that led to a landing platform used for supply shipments. Inside, Decimus sat in his cell, behind a magnetically locked door with an energy shield.

As Decimus was lost in his thoughts, the clattering of a tray snapped him back to reality.

"Eat up," the guard sneered.

Decimus smiled and said, "Today is my last day here."

The guard laughed, "You'll never escape from here. You should be grateful that you're not forced to fight like the other prisoners."

Decimus' eyes narrowed as the guard collapsed to the ground, gasping for air. He then retrieved the guard's keycard, unlocking the door and deactivating the energy shield.

Security droids, armed with electric batons and shields, soon arrived.

"Prisoner 522, stand down," they commanded.

Decimus, reacting quickly, released a Repulsion, sending them flying.

Alarms sounded as he picked up an electric baton and shield from one of the droids. He then ran down the hallway, his feet echoing against the steel floor. As he turned a corner, security drones descended from the ceiling, swarming him. Decimus raised his riot shield and charged forward, soon arriving at the control room. He then released a stream of lightning, creating an energy surge. The lights turned red as auxiliary power was engaged.

As Decimus reached the outer shield, it shimmered with an ethereal blue light. Decimus outstretched his hands as the air around him began to vibrate. He then channeled all of his power into a Repulsion, releasing a shockwave of lightning. Decimus charged through the shield.

He quickly ran toward the landing platform, scanning for a shuttle. He then noticed a Beta Interceptor, known for its speed and maneuverability.

Climbing inside, the cockpit lit up as the engines roared to life. Decimus soared through the atmosphere, but soon realized he was not alone.

Lieutenant Zhang, one of the pilots pursuing Decimus, hailed the Roman cruiser ahead.

"Captain Aulus, this is Lieutenant Zhang of the Yuan Empire. Prisoner Decimus has escaped and commandeered one of our fighters. Serial number ZR-1138. He's moving out of the upper atmosphere toward your position," the pilot reported.

Captain Aulus informed Admiral Leonidas of the situation.

"Activate the tractor beam and prepare to detain him," Admiral Leonidas ordered. "This is Admiral Leonidas. Break off the attack!"

As the fighters broke off, Decimus noticed the Roman cruiser. The cruiser then activated its tractor beam, pulling his interceptor into the hangar. Decimus leapt out of the cockpit and dashed down the hallway, evading the Roman soldiers.

He then climbed into an escape pod and jettisoned it toward Earth.

The Roman cruiser fired at the escape pod, but Decimus evaded their attacks, escaping unharmed.

Admiral Leonidas watched as Decimus disappeared from their sensors. He slammed his fist on the console and said, "I'll be in my quarters."

Once there, he activated his transmitter.

The warden, appearing as a hologram, said, "This isn't a good time. I just had a prisoner escape."

"I know," Admiral Leonidas replied. "We tried to detain him, but he escaped. Why didn't you follow protocol?"

"I didn't want to escalate the situation," the warden responded.

Leonidas replied, "You should've alerted Cohort 13. Now I'll have to inform them and Grand Admiral Tarquinius. You're lucky it was me up here and not some other admiral who doesn't know about Decimus, or your fighters would've been destroyed."

He then ended the transmission. After explaining the situation to Cohort 13, he was transferred to Vincentius, the Cohort 13 Director.

"We're escalating the situation to priority one," said Vincentius. "I want the trajectory of the escape pod and a list of possible headings. I'll contact the Bureau of National Security to alert local law enforcement about the possible landing zones. I'll also need a full report and any recordings you have of the prisoner. He's an international criminal and is considered threat level one, so we need to deal with him before any politicians find out about this. Grand Admiral Tarquinius has already been informed and should arrive at your location within the hour."

Admiral Leonidas nodded before ending the transmission. "This is why I didn't want to inform Cohort 13," he muttered.

Back at Cohort 13 Headquarters, agents were bustling about, delivering files and information regarding Decimus. One of the agents spoke up, "Sir, I recommend contacting General Ireneus and informing him of the situation with his brother."

Another agent replied, "Ship transit logs indicate that he left Earth several days ago bound for Mars. It'll be difficult to contact him until he returns."

Vincentius sighed, "I'll have to convene the council if we can't find him by the end of the day. To avoid that unfortunate outcome, I want to deploy every ship we have to guard the space lanes. Call up our reserve ships from Jupiter Station."

Meanwhile, Decimus' pod shot across the sky like a comet, fire trailing behind him. He rapidly approached the Financial District of Caralis, narrowly dodging the skyscrapers before ejecting the lid of the pod and leaping out onto a nearby ledge. The pod crashed into the Forum, creating a massive fireball as many people looked up. However, Decimus remained elusive. He made his way down the skyscraper by taking a service elevator and escaped into the street below.

Faunus was at the table talking to his mom when they heard a knock at the door. When his mom opened it, she saw Decimus standing there, smiling. His gray prison jumpsuit was tattered, and his gray beard and hair were unkempt. His face was coarse, and he had tattoos on his arms.

Decimus smiled and said, "It's nice to see you again."

His mom tried to close the door but Decimus put his hand on it and said, "Aurora, can't I stay a little while? I did escape prison after all."

Aurora replied, "Leave, no one wants you here."

Decimus, seeing Faunus, had tears well up in his eyes. Faunus looked up and asked, "Dad?"

Decimus nodded as he ran into Faunus' arms. They embraced tightly, and as they pulled apart, his gaze fell upon Faunus' unusual eye. He said in a gruff voice, "What the hell is that?"

Faunus laughed and said, "It's called the Optoculo. It's the eye Eamon Pompeanus possessed."

"Is that so," Decimus said, his voice filled with pride. Faunus went on to explain the Optoculo's abilities and its potential.

"I felt your presence the other day, and that's what inspired me to escape," said Decimus.

Aurora scoffed, "So now, you've decided to care about him."

At that moment, Uncle Ireneus walked in carrying a vase of flowers. When he saw Decimus, he dropped the vase on the ground. After a brief moment, Uncle Ireneus said, "Decimus?"

Decimus scoffed and looked away.

Uncle Iren continued, "After all this time, you still hate me."

Decimus then looked back at him and said, "Yes, I do. You betrayed me by refusing to join me that night. If you were there, we could've dealt a devastating blow to the government."

Uncle Ireneus sighed and said, "Decimus, you've always been rash. You were more interested in causing chaos than actually bringing about change. I serve the government to protect our family."

Decimus shouted, "You serve murderers."

Uncle Iren replied, "I advocate for change in Cohort 13 and in the military. I have made significant progress by working on the inside as opposed to inciting violence."

Decimus shouted, "This government needs to be deposed!"

Uncle Iren replied, "The time for that to occur has not yet come and terrorizing people only causes more problems."

Faunus then spoke, saying, "What is going on with you two?"

Decimus laughed and said, "I'm not surprised your uncle never told you about how he's a coward and a traitor."

Uncle Ireneus replied, "I'm no traitor, Decimus, for I'm true to what I believe."

Faunus then looked at his uncle with a saddened look on his face.

Uncle Iren sighed and said, "I suppose it's time you heard the story of what happened to your father." He then looked at Decimus who nodded in agreement as they all sat down to reminisce over the events that led to Decimus' imprisonment.

Chapter Four

Nexus

Apollo Station had numerous concentric rings, with hallways connecting the various modules. In the center of the station, a large tablinum provided a breathtaking view of Earth.

Inside the tablinum, several semicircle tables were arranged. The floor bore the emblem of Nexus, an illustration of Earth pierced by a sword.

Admiral Leonidas was the first to enter, his boots echoing through the room, followed by Vincentius, Director of Cohort 13.

Next came Lutisius the Miser, CEO of Lutisian Bank, wearing a golden toga and white tunic.

Lutisius the Immortal, founder of numerous pharmaceutical companies, entered after him. He had brown hair and wore a purple toga.

Then came Lutisius the Merciless, chairman of the Mining Syndicate.

Lord Chao, owner of a weapons research company, followed, with Shi and Yan, prominent politicians from the Yuan Empire, entering next.

Prime Minister Guo of the Yuan Empire then entered.

Grand Admiral Tarquinius arrived with his Praetorian Guards. He wore a white military uniform adorned with medals.

Tarquinius announced, "Please welcome the Vice President of the Roman Republic and leader of Nexus, Constantine."

Constantine, wearing a pink-striped suit and red tie, declared, "Greetings everyone. Apologies for being late. Let's get started."

Yan said, "He always makes a production out of everything."

Lutisius the Immortal asked, "Why are we all here?"

Constantine replied, "Decimus has escaped prison."

Lutisius the Miser laughed and said, "Who cares? I can have an assassin eliminate him by tomorrow."

Admiral Leonidas retorted, "It's not that easy."

Prime Minister Guo spoke up, "This unfortunately happened under my watch since he was imprisoned in our facility. However, there was no indication that he was planning an escape; it just happened."

Vincentius added, "Precisely, it did just happen. It's almost as if he was suddenly motivated by someone to escape."

Lutisius the Merciless suggested, "I can always use a strong slave; why not send him to my mine?"

Admiral Leonidas countered, "I recommend imprisoning him in our Cohort 13 compound in Frigoria."

Constantine said, "First, we need to capture him. As for how, I already have a plan."

Lord Chao inquired, "Do you? Well, let's hear it then."

Constantine suggested, "Lord Vespasian is an expert on Knights. We should have him deal with Decimus."

Tarquinius then activated the transmitter. A moment later, Vespasian appeared as a hologram.

The council members explained the situation to Vespasian. After listening, Vespasian said, "Constantine, come to my compound so we can discuss this." The transmission then ended.

Constantine instructed, "We'll reconvene once I've spoken with Lord Vespasian."

Lutisius the Immortal said, "I'm accompanying you."

Constantine replied, "I wouldn't recommend going with me."

Lord Chao added, "I'm going too."

Grand Admiral Tarquinius said, "Since everyone else is going, I'll come along too."

Constantine replied, "Very well, you can all come."

Shortly after the meeting ended, Constantine's Nebula Class cruiser made its departure from Apollo Station. Within an hour, they arrived at Kuiper Station."

Kuiper Station, located near the Kuiper Belt beyond Neptune, consisted of numerous concentric rings with the outermost ring used for docking and the innermost ring inhabited by half a million people. The station was dim, with the buildings barely visible under the faint light of the distant Sun.

Constantine spoke, "This station used to be inhabited by miners and researchers, who worked in the Kuiper Belt. Since the mining operations were abandoned in favor of utilizing the closer Asteroid Belt, it became very poor. Eventually, it was no longer used as a trading outpost with the construction of Poseidon Station near Neptune. As a result, it descended into lawlessness and became known as a place where those who don't want to be found go. Over the years, many Pompeani have used this station as a source of slave labor. It's estimated that around 50,000 people were trafficked from this location. However, in recent years, the trafficking has stopped and any Pompeani who come to this place never return. This is all a result of Lord Vespasian. Because of this, Kuiper Station fashions Lord Vespasian as its unofficial leader."

As they docked, a man in a dark cloak approached and said, "Lord Vespasian is expecting you."

They followed him through the station, eventually reaching the surface of the ring. The sight was unusual, with the ring curving above them. They approached a fortress constructed of black stone, with pillars of dark red granite. Guards in black armor with red visors, wielding Spathas, stood outside.

Inside, they saw four Pompeani chained to poles, two with the Spectoculo and two with the Potestoculo, an eye that is considered extremely rare within the Pompeanus Clan.

Lord Vespasian greeted them, "Welcome, Constantine and members of Nexus."

Vespasian had dark hair and he wore a black suit with a dark fur trim.

Lutisius the Immortal demanded, "Why are they being tortured?"

Lord Vespasian replied calmly, "I'm conducting research."

Lutisius the Immortal, enraged, shouted, "This is madness, Vespasian!"

Vespasian interjected, "This may appear to be madness, but my research is necessary to understand their eyes."

The Immortal replied, "I couldn't care less. Release them immediately!"

Vespasian smiled and replied, "You're welcome to try to free them."

The Immortal unsheathed his Gladius. He then consumed a pill that made his muscles bulge and his eyes dilate.

Vespasian said, "Your technology pales in comparison to true power."

Lutisius the Immortal swung his Gladius at Vespasian, who dodged the attack with ease. He then unleashed his lightning, causing him to fall to the ground, writhing in pain.

Lutisius the Immortal, struggling to stand, pressed his attack, but Vespasian remained unfazed.

Vespasian warned, "This is your last chance to back down."

Lutisius the Immortal shouted in defiance, "I will not yield to you!"

Lord Vespasian said, "Lightning Waltz," as he created a stream of lightning between his hands. Suddenly, Vespasian appeared behind him, electrocuting him.

The room fell silent. Constantine, who had been smiling, now appeared frightened after witnessing Vespasian's power.

Vespasian said, "Apologies, if you would follow me."

Vespasian then led them into the tablinum. They gathered around a large table made of dark oak wood, with ancient runes carved into it.

Vespasian said, "Decimus has impressive abilities but he's not dangerous. I paid him a visit when he was in prison but he proved no interest to me. I was more interested in how he learned to use his powers and if there were others like him. Unfortunately, I was never able to get an answer."

Lord Chao interjected, "What do you suggest we do?"

Vespasian said, "First, we must understand what motivates him, and then we can devise a strategy to eliminate him."

Grand Admiral Tarquinius responded, "We've already identified a weakness, his family."

Vespasian, curious, asked, "Does Decimus have a son?"

Tarquinius answered, "Yes, his name is Faunus."

Lord Vespasian smiled and said, "This is no longer your concern. I'll see to it that Decimus is eliminated."

As he said this, Silvius entered, his left eye now appearing different than before.

Constantine asked, "What eye is that?"

Vespasian replied, "The Transoculo, the most powerful of all the eyes inherited from Eamon Pompeanus." He added, "My apprentice will handle this, but first, I need you to reconvene Nexus so I can speak with everyone. There's no need for you to attend the meeting. Once I've met with them, I'll give you further instructions."

Back on Earth, Faunus listened intently to his father recount the story that led to his imprisonment.

Decimus began, "Years ago, I was part of a group known as Libertus. We advocated for social reform, but our methods were... unconventional. We orchestrated acts of violence against the government to rally others to our cause. Our most infamous attack was on Luna City, in which we declared the region an independent territory from the Roman Republic. However, the government retaliated and regained control over the city. Ironically, our numbers grew as a result of our loss."

He paused, his gaze distant as he relived the past. "I went to your uncle and asked him to rally his men for a coup against the government. He warned me that not all of his men would side with us and that we would be endangering the Roman Republic. He feared that the Yuan Empire could take advantage of the instability and conquer Rome."

Decimus sighed, "I ignored his advice. I led my men in an attack against Cohort 13 Headquarters in Rome, hoping to seize weapons and ships. However, the attack was a disaster. The enemy knew we were coming. The area was soon lit up with energy weapons as Omega Cruisers began bombarding us."

His voice hardened, "I then revealed my powers. I lifted up a tank and toppled it over before retrieving my Spatha and deflecting every projectile shot at me. I electrified the ground, neutralizing several dozen soldiers before we retreated into the compound, rigged with explosives. I awoke to the sight of the sun rising over a devastated Rome as thousands lay dead around me."

Decimus' voice dropped to a whisper, "I tried to escape, but I could barely stand. I was then apprehended by Admiral Tarquinius. I later learned that your uncle had revealed the identities of our sympathizers and launched an investigation to find our remaining hideouts. Around 300 more of our men were captured, and the last of Libertus was destroyed. Your uncle abandoned me that night and betrayed us."

Faunus sat in silence, his mind reeling from the revelations. His uncle stood there, head bowed, unable to meet his gaze.

Faunus asked, "How could you do this, Uncle?"

Uncle Iren replied, "I did it to protect our family. I hope you can forgive me."

Faunus shouted, "No, you're a coward! Why wouldn't you help him?"

Aurora, disappointed, said, "Faunus."

Faunus then stood up and ran outside into the street. His family repeatedly called for him but he was already gone.

Meanwhile, Nexus gathered at Apollo Station.

"I can't believe we've been summoned here again," grumbled Senator Augusta.

"This is an outrage!" shouted General Laberius. "Vespasian has no right to call us here like this."

"I agree," replied Lutisius the Miser.

Prime Minister Guo asked, "Since when did we take orders from Vespasian?"

Vincentius replied, "We don't. Constantine requested that we meet with him."

A Pompeani guard then announced, "Lord Vespasian's ship has arrived."

A few moments later, a man entered the room. He had black hair and brown eyes, and he wore a black suit with a golden chain around his neck. In his hand, he held a Gladius.

Lutisius the Merciless asked, "Who are you?"

The main remained silent.

Prime Minister Guo ordered, "Seize him," as Pompeani guards surrounded him.

Mortus said, "Lord Vespasian sent me."

Vespasian then entered the room and said, "Excellent, I see you're all here."

Vincentius asked, "What do you want, Vespasian?"

Vespasian replied, "I want to inform you that Nexus is hereby disbanded."

Lutisius the Miser laughed, "I don't know who you think you are, but we will not tolerate such insolence."

Vespasian smiled and responded, "Your rule is at an end."

Mortus swung his sword, beheading the Pompeani guards surrounding him.

A woman with blond hair, wearing a black dress, then entered the room. In her hand, she held a spear attached to a metal string. A large man with brown hair, wearing a white robe, followed behind, wielding an ax.

Vespasian introduced them, "This is Valeria and Maximus."

Mortus then dashed at Lutisius the Miser, stabbing him in the chest. He channeled lightning into his sword and stabbed the floor, creating a shockwave of lightning, sending Lutisus the Merciless flying.

Meanwhile, Maximus and Valeria engaged the Pompeani guards.

Vincentius aimed an energy weapon at Vespasian, but Mortus threw a Pugio at him, slicing his arm. Cohort 13 agents quickly surrounded him as

Vespasian turned to face them. He unleashed his lightning, causing them to fall to the ground, writhing in pain.

Vincentius, gritting his teeth, said, "You betrayed us."

Vespasian waved his hand, snapping his neck.

He walked towards Lutisius the Merciless and taunted, "You lasted a lot longer than the Immortal. Ironic, that he died so easily."

"You bastard," he cursed.

Vespasian nodded as Mortus stabbed him.

He then unleashed his lightning at the Nexus banner above the door, lighting it on fire. As they departed, Vespasian placed a bomb on the floor. Within a few minutes, the bomb exploded, decimating Apollo Station.

On board his ship, Vespasian activated his transmitter. Constantine looked up as a hologram of Vespasian appeared.

"How did the meeting go?" Constantine asked.

"The entire Nexus is dead," Vespasian replied.

Constantine's eyes widened as he remained silent for a moment. Finally, he spoke, "Praetoria eliminated Nexus? Why?"

"Maybe it's because I can't stand the look of Pompeani or the thought of having to listen to them," Vespasian said, disdain filling his voice.

Constantine smiled and said, "This move will turn the Roman Republic, the Yuan Empire, and Pompeani against you. That would be the case anyways, if we didn't redirect the blame. I understand that Prime Minister

Guo was there. We can take responsibility for the attack as an assassination attempt. The Roman Republic will deal with the fallout."

Vespasian replied, "I knew you'd have a plan to cover this up." He added, "I want you to attack Caralis. We need chaos to apprehend Faunus without anyone noticing."

Constantine's eyebrows shot up, but he quickly regained his composure. "Normally I'd be hesitant, but since you did me a favor by eliminating several of my rivals within the government, I'm more than willing to do this. I'll entrust the capture of Faunus to you."

Back on Earth, Faunus sat on a ledge overlooking Caralis. Several hours had passed and the sun was beginning to set.

Faunus thought, "Why would Uncle do that?"

He then heard footsteps and turned around to see Decimus standing behind him.

Decimus said, "I've been looking for you. I'm glad to see that you're alright."

Faunus turned away and said, "I want to be alone."

Decimus sat next to him and said, "Your uncle and I have our problems, but don't let that affect you." He asked, "Do you want to hear my plan?"

Faunus looked up with a hint of curiosity and asked, "What plan?"

Decimus replied, "To overthrow the government, we need to rally others to our cause. To do this, we need to send a message through the Communications Tower on the island."

Faunus replied, "How?"

Decimus smiled and said, "I still have some friends who work for the Roman Republic Communications Outlet. They could broadcast the message."

Faunus asked, "What would I do?"

Decimus replied, "I'm glad you asked. You'll create a distraction to divert attention away from the Communications Tower."

Decimus retrieved his Gladius and showed it to Faunus. He said, "This is my secondary sword. Unfortunately, I lost my main sword after I was arrested. Hopefully, you'll have one just like this one day."

Faunus looked at the sword with amazement and said, "I hope so too."

The two then hugged as the sun went down over the horizon.

Later, they arrived at a bar near the beach.

Decimus walked in and greeted everyone, "It's been a while."

"Decimus!" they exclaimed.

"Friends, it's good to see you again!" Decimus said, clapping a few of them on the back. He then gestured to Faunus, "This is my son, Faunus."

Decimus announced, "I've come here to share my plan, one that could change the course of our future. We need to send a message, a rallying cry to those who still believe in freedom. We need to broadcast this message to the entire Roman Republic."

Several people in the room exchanged uneasy glances. One man spoke up, "Decimus, that's a dangerous game you're playing. The government won't take kindly to such a move."

"I know the risks," Decimus replied. "But we must act. A few of you still work for the Communications Outlet, don't you?"

A few people nodded. "We're on board," one of them said. "We'll help you send the message."

With the plan set in motion, Decimus and Faunus sat down for a drink. Decimus began to tell stories of old battles and adventures to the crowd while Faunus drifted off to sleep in a corner of the bar.

The next morning, Decimus' voice woke up Faunus. "You ready? Today's the day!" Faunus rubbed his eyes and sat up to see Decimus with a few of his friends.

"I want you to go to the Forum and create a distraction," Decimus instructed. "Make sure you create enough chaos to divert as many guards as possible away from the Communications Tower. I'll head to the Cohort 13 Complex and cause more trouble. These distractions should allow my friends here to get in and transmit a message without being seen."

"What's the message?" Faunus asked.

"We recorded it last night while you were sleeping. It's good, trust me." Decimus replied, handing him a transmitter. "Keep this on you so we can communicate during the mission."

Back at the house, Uncle Ireneus said, "I hope Faunus is alright; he still hasn't returned," concern evident in his voice.

"Decimus went out looking for him last night, but knowing him, he's probably at a bar. I'm sure Faunus is alright though. They'll be back soon," Aurora reassured him.

Meanwhile, Faunus arrived at the Forum. "How do I create a distraction?" he wondered aloud. Seeing a market stand selling oils, he grabbed a jug and ran. He thought, "Stealing something should draw attention."

However, his plan went awry when he tripped and fell into a food stand. The oil spilled, catching fire on an open flame, engulfing the tent. Everyone began to panic as Roman Police quickly arrived at the scene.

A shopkeeper pointed at Faunus and shouted, "That's him! He's the one!"

A Roman Police Officer told him, "You're under arrest for disruption of the peace."

Faunus, without thinking, extended his hands, launching him across the Forum.

Meanwhile, Decimus made his way towards the Complex. As he walked through an alley, he entered a large open area with skyscrapers on each side. In the center was a fountain. All of a sudden, he heard a voice, "You must be Decimus."

Decimus turned around to see a figure concealed in a dark cloak. He asked, "Who are you?"

The figure replied, "My name is Silvius." Without warning, Silvius dashed at Decimus, who quickly retrieved his Gladius to block Silvius' blade. The two stood, their blades locked.

Decimus leapt back and said, "You must be Vespasian's apprentice."

Silvius replied, "You must be Faunus' dad. I was really hoping to fight Faunus, but I'll settle for you."

Decimus glared and channeled a stream of lightning through his sword at Silvius, who disappeared, only to reappear a moment later. Decimus said to himself, "He must possess the Optoculo."

Silvius undid his black cloak and looked at Decimus, who was now beginning to sweat. Silvius then appeared behind Decimus, concealing his presence before stabbing him. Decimus let out a Repulsion, a shockwave of lightning, but Silvius dodged it.

Silvius blinked, and a spear appeared in his hand, which he threw at Decimus, who deflected it. Silvius launched another spear but Decimus extended his hand, freezing the spear in midair. Silvius continued to materialize spears and launch them at Decimus.

Decimus released a Repulsion, intercepting the spears, causing them to fall to the ground. Silvius charged at Decimus, who sidestepped his attack. In an instant, Silvius reappeared above him, concealing his presence before materializing a spear and throwing it at him. The spear gashed Decimus' back. Silvius attempted to stab him but Decimus parried his attack with his Gladius.

Silvius disengaged, as several Omega Cruisers appeared in the sky, along with Grand Admiral Tarquinius' Titan Cruiser. Decimus heard explosions as fighters roared overhead.

Decimus started launching stones at Silvius, who blinked, transporting all of the projectiles into the Pompeanus Dimension. Silvius then materialized the projectiles and blasted them back at Decimus, causing him to fall to the ground.

Decimus then put his hands together, preparing to use the Resonance Ability as he said, "Resonance."

Silvius quickly closed his eye with the Spectoculo. He continued walking forward, unfazed. "I possess the Transoculo, which allows me to see through your illusions," he said as he threw a spear at Decimus, pinning him to the ground.

Silvius stood over him and said, "I hope Faunus proves to be more interesting."

Decimus smiled, blood on his lips. "I know he will be. My son shall surpass both of us."

Silvius then channeled plasma into his sword and stabbed Decimus through the chest.

The sky gradually darkened as it began to rain. Silvius tilted his head upwards, feeling the raindrops against his skin, before slowly walking towards the fountain. He stood there, his eyes fixed on the rippling surface of the water, gazing at the distorted reflection of himself.

Silvius said to himself, "I wonder what it's like to have a father."

After some time, he closed his eyes in an attempt to sense Faunus. He then smiled and said, "Found you."

Back in the Forum, Faunus and the Roman Police tried to evacuate everyone.

An energy bomb was then dropped by a Gamma Bomber. Faunus leapt up and blasted it back at the bomber, destroying it in an explosion. Everyone looked up with astonishment as Faunus landed on a tent, which collapsed under his weight. As he stumbled out of the debris, everyone began to cheer for him.

Faunus tried to call Decimus, but there was no response. Panicking, he called Decimus' friends at the Communications Tower.

"We can't get a hold of Decimus," one of his friends replied.

Faunus responded, "I haven't been able to either." He asked, "Were you able to get into the building?"

"Yes, we got in without anyone noticing. We're ready to transmit, but we wanted to check with Decimus first," one of them replied.

"Do it," Faunus said. "I have to take care of something." He then ran towards home, his heart pounding.

A few moments later, a message rang out over the speakers in Sardinia, "My name is Decimus Virelius, a patriot fighting for you. We've let our freedoms be taken from us for so long that we no longer know how to live as free men."

Meanwhile, on Grand Admiral Tarquinius' Cruiser. A communications officer reported, "Sir, this message is being broadcasted to the entire Roman Republic on all channels."

Grand Admiral Tarquinius ordered, "Locate the source and prepare to fire on it."

Silvius, hearing the message, raced towards the Communications Tower. Looking up, he transported himself on top of the building. He then channeled lightning into his sword and began slicing the support beams of the communications array.

Meanwhile, the message continued to broadcast, "This fight is not just for us but for our children. I have a son, and I want him to grow up in a better world. We are responsible for how the world is now. Therefore, it is our duty to rise up and stand together, as one."

At that moment, Silvius sliced the last support beam, and the structure came crashing down. A garbled sound was emitted from the tower for a moment before going silent.

through your illusions," he said as he threw a spear at Decimus, pinning him to the ground.

Silvius stood over him and said, "I hope Faunus proves to be more interesting."

Decimus smiled, blood on his lips. "I know he will be. My son shall surpass both of us."

Silvius then channeled plasma into his sword and stabbed Decimus through the chest.

The sky gradually darkened as it began to rain. Silvius tilted his head upwards, feeling the raindrops against his skin, before slowly walking towards the fountain. He stood there, his eyes fixed on the rippling surface of the water, gazing at the distorted reflection of himself.

Silvius said to himself, "I wonder what it's like to have a father."

After some time, he closed his eyes in an attempt to sense Faunus. He then smiled and said, "Found you."

Back in the Forum, Faunus and the Roman Police tried to evacuate everyone.

An energy bomb was then dropped by a Gamma Bomber. Faunus leapt up and blasted it back at the bomber, destroying it in an explosion. Everyone looked up with astonishment as Faunus landed on a tent, which collapsed under his weight. As he stumbled out of the debris, everyone began to cheer for him.

Faunus tried to call Decimus, but there was no response. Panicking, he called Decimus' friends at the Communications Tower.

"We can't get a hold of Decimus," one of his friends replied.

Faunus responded, "I haven't been able to either." He asked, "Were you able to get into the building?"

"Yes, we got in without anyone noticing. We're ready to transmit, but we wanted to check with Decimus first," one of them replied.

"Do it," Faunus said. "I have to take care of something." He then ran towards home, his heart pounding.

A few moments later, a message rang out over the speakers in Sardinia, "My name is Decimus Virelius, a patriot fighting for you. We've let our freedoms be taken from us for so long that we no longer know how to live as free men."

Meanwhile, on Grand Admiral Tarquinius' Cruiser. A communications officer reported, "Sir, this message is being broadcasted to the entire Roman Republic on all channels."

Grand Admiral Tarquinius ordered, "Locate the source and prepare to fire on it."

Silvius, hearing the message, raced towards the Communications Tower. Looking up, he transported himself on top of the building. He then channeled lightning into his sword and began slicing the support beams of the communications array.

Meanwhile, the message continued to broadcast, "This fight is not just for us but for our children. I have a son, and I want him to grow up in a better world. We are responsible for how the world is now. Therefore, it is our duty to rise up and stand together, as one."

At that moment, Silvius sliced the last support beam, and the structure came crashing down. A garbled sound was emitted from the tower for a moment before going silent.

Faunus said to himself, tears forming in his eyes, "We did it, Dad."

Meanwhile, on the Titan Cruiser, Grand Admiral Tarquinius demanded a status report as officers frantically ran about the room. Another communications officer reported, "Sir, the transmission has been cut off."

"Excellent," he replied. "Let's continue our bombardment."

Back at his house, Faunus found his mom searching for him.

Faunus shouted, "Mom!"

Aurora hugged him, tears forming in her eyes.

"Mom, I was so worried about you," said Faunus.

"I was worried about you too. I'm glad you're alright," she replied.

"Did you hear our message?" asked Faunus.

"I did," Aurora responded. "I'm so proud of you."

Faunus said, "Come on, Mom, we need to leave."

They started to run towards the business district, but suddenly, they heard a loud explosion as the sky lit up behind them. A fighter then roared overhead.

Another incendiary bomb was dropped. As it began to fall, Uncle Ireneus appeared and said, "Sophus Mode," launching the bomb back at the fighter.

Uncle Ireneus stood, energy surging around him, his entire body glowing white. Aboard the Titan, an officer asked, "What was that?" Another officer informed, "Sir, I believe someone redirected one of our bombs."

Grand Admiral Tarquinius instructed, "Have our AI analyze what happened."

A moment later, the officer replied, "We've identified the individual as General Ireneus..." At this, the entire bridge went silent. Tarquinius ordered, "Get me Constantine. Now!"

An officer reported, "Sir, another fighter just went down."

Back on the ground, Uncle Iren was launching lightning at nearby fighters. The Omega Cruiser above continued to drop bombs on Ireneus. However, he remained unfazed.

Two more high-yield energy bombs were dropped, which Uncle Ireneus froze and blasted back at the Omega Cruiser. In an instant, the Omega Cruiser erupted into a fireball. Uncle Ireneus froze the debris in midair before slowly lowering it to the ground.

Everyone aboard the Titan Cruiser was terrified.

An officer informed Tarquinius, "Vice President Constantine is unavailable."

Tarquinius, annoyed, said, "I'll deal with this myself." He commanded, "Charge the energy cannon and prepare to reposition the cruiser."

Meanwhile, Faunus watched from a nearby building. The energy cannon on Tarquinius' ship glowed as it prepared to fire. On board his cruiser, an officer reported, "The weapon is fully charged, Sir."

"Fire," Grand Admiral Tarquinius ordered.

At that moment, an energy beam shot out at Uncle Ireneus. He said to himself, "If I'm unable to stop this attack, my family and everyone in this city will die." He then extended his hands in an attempt to absorb the blast.

The blast was overwhelming, illuminating the area in a bright flash of light. Uncle Ireneus stood firm, pouring every ounce of his power into absorbing the attack as Faunus stared in disbelief.

Uncle Iren then moved his fists together and released a Repulsion, discharging the energy back at the Titan Cruiser. In an instant, the cruiser glowed blue as the blast slammed into it. The resulting explosion created a shockwave, shattering windows throughout the city.

Uncle Ireneus then looked back at Faunus and smiled as the remaining energy exploded around him. Faunus saw a cloud of smoke rising from where his Uncle had stood. His right eye began to pulse as tears streamed down his face. His eye then transformed into the Transoculo.

"Uncle!" he shouted, his voice filled with grief.

Chapter Five

The General

The next day, protesters gathered in the Forum, burning Roman flags and shouting, "Death to Rome!"

The Senator of Sardinia, an older man with gray hair, stood on a hover tank. "Citizens of Sardinia," he began. "I understand your anger. The Yuan Empire will be brought to justice for this heinous act."

However, his words fell on deaf ears. The anger of the crowd intensified as Roman Police struggled to keep back the protestors.

Away from the chaos, Faunus searched through the debris for his uncle. "Uncle Ireneus!" he shouted, his voice hoarse. Nearby, his mother shouted, "Ireneus! Where are you?"

Meanwhile, in Rome, Cohort 13 agents rushed in and out of Constatine's office, delivering reports.

Suddenly, the noise was interrupted by the sound of a Sigma Shuttle landing outside. The shuttle doors opened, as Cohort 13 agents stepped out. In their midst was a handcuffed person with a blindfold over their eyes.

As they brought him into Constantine's office, he quickly ordered everyone out. They then removed the blindfold.

"To think you were a Knight all along, General Ireneus," Constantine remarked.

Constantine shouted, "You destroyed two cruisers and killed Grand Admiral Tarquinius!"

"If we're keeping track, I also destroyed a few fighters," replied Ireneus.

A Cohort 13 agent slammed his face into the desk. Constantine leaned in and said, "If it were up to me, I would kill you right here, but someone else wants you."

Silvius then entered his office. Ireneus looked up and said, "I see you awakened the Transoculo, very impressive."

Silvius scoffed, "Does my master really want this guy?"

Constantine cautioned, "Don't underestimate him. He's dangerous."

Silvius shrugged, "Just don't annoy me."

Ireneus smiled and said, "I'll try not to."

Later on, they arrived at Kuiper Station. As Ireneus was led through the station, he noticed the cramped living conditions and dilapidated buildings. He said to himself, "It's still rough, but somehow, it seems better than when I was last here." He then put his hands together and stopped for a brief moment.

Silvius and Mortus, seeing this, swung their swords at him. Ireneus, reacting quickly, blocked one with his foot and the other in between his hands.

Mortus threatened, "Don't try that again."

They continued walking and soon arrived at Vespasian's compound. Vespasian greeted him, "Welcome, Master Ireneus."

Ireneus replied, "Pleasure to make your acquaintance. If I may ask, who are you?"

Vespasian replied, "I'm no one. I have no real significance, but my quest, that is what is truly important."

Ireneus asked, "Your quest?"

Vespasian replied, "Yes, my quest to unravel the mysteries of nature and the power surrounding the Knights of Rome."

Ireneus advised, "Those who seek everything will inevitably lose everything."

Vespasian responded, "We shall see."

Ireneus was led into the tablinum, a large space with a tall ceiling, lit by a chandelier. A dark wooden table, marked with ancient symbols, stood in the center of the room.

Silvius and Mortus positioned themselves behind Ireneus as he took a seat across from Vespasian.

Vespasian said, "You destroyed Grand Admiral Tarquinius' Cruiser by redirecting the energy blast. Containing and redirecting that much energy is beyond the capabilities of any Knight I've read about, except for one. Long ago, a Knight named Marcus developed an ability known as Sophus Mode. This allowed him to take in energy from his surroundings to amplify his own power. How did you learn this?"

Uncle Ireneus took a deep breath, his eyes distant as he recalled a painful past. "Many years ago, I led a campaign against the Yuan Empire. At this time, I had no knowledge of the Knights of Rome nor their philosophy."

He continued, "I believed I was unstoppable. Eventually, my army, consisting of three legions, went up against the defensive forces of Hua'an. The siege lasted for several months. The mounting losses, lack of reinforcements, and constant fighting had a severe effect on my men.

Eventually, our supplies were cut off as the passage we had created was recaptured. Around this time, the Yuan Empire began to use satellites with directed energy weapons to ignite fires throughout our campsite."

Ireneus paused as tears began to form in his eyes. "One day, I returned from the front to find that the fortification with my wife and newborn child in it had been burned. I was devastated and I ordered an immediate retreat. A division of 500 men including myself remained behind. The battle was intense and we were soon overwhelmed by Yuan forces."

He paused again before continuing. "I managed to escape on horseback. I rode for days, eventually collapsing from exhaustion. I must have been near a monastery since I was found by a group of Buddhist monks. I soon recovered but my mind was still in turmoil. It was there I learned how to manipulate energy. After a few months of living at the monastery, I departed for Rome. After returning, I was considered a war hero but I did not deserve such praise."

He looked down and said, "My ambition cost me my family and so many of my men. I eventually realized that the Roman Republic had become corrupt and I sought to reform it. I also began to learn more about the Knights of Rome and eventually imparted this knowledge onto my brother, Decimus. Regrettably, this too was a mistake."

Ireneus asked, "Is Decimus dead?"

Silvius answered, "Yes, he is."

Ireneus, his voice heavy with sorrow, responded, "That explains why I couldn't sense him using Sophus Mode."

Vespasian said, "It was nothing personal, merely a task we were assigned. I, too, have known loss."

He then recalled his past, "I was born on Kuiper Station, in a dilapidated dwelling. Tragically, my mother died shortly after my birth. My father, though present, was a poor excuse for a parent and a habitual drunk. He worked as a spaceship mechanic, but with Kuiper Station receiving less traffic, work was hard to find. Eventually, his drinking led to a fight with a coworker, costing him his job.

Desperation soon set in. Food became scarce, and our situation caught the attention of wealthy Pompeani in search of cheap labor. Kuiper, with its lack of official records, became a popular spot for human trafficking. At 14, my father sold me to a Pompeani merchant for drinking money.

I still remember the day he left me in the hangar. I, along with hundreds of other children, was transported to a cobalt mine in Aegyptus. Although the territory was under the jurisdiction of the Roman Republic, it was effectively ruled by Lutisius the Brutal.

Life in the mines was hellish. Over ten thousand people, including myself, worked in horrific conditions. Our rudimentary shelters, made of wood and straw, housed many people. Clean water was a rarity, with one basin being shared among fifty people. Disease ran rampant, and our meager rations were often contaminated with sand or dirt. The scorching sun drained us, with dehydration being a constant threat.

Yet, amidst this misery, I found comfort. I met Mortus, although at the time he went by a different name, and several others: Maximus, Valeria, Romulus, Cassius, Diana, Titus, Vulcan, Brutus, Julio, Horatius, Justinius, and Livia. Together, we formed a family, sharing our meager resources and looking out for one another.

As time went on, I grew closer to Livia. We often spent our nights together, gazing at the stars. One day, we decided to sneak into Lutisius' compound, where we discovered a library. Among the ancient texts, one stood out, a black leather book adorned with a sword, written in an unfamiliar language. I decided to take it. Just as we were about to leave, a guard entered and spotted Livia.

He seized her and dragged her off. I was too afraid to intervene, terrified of being caught as well. The next day, Lutisius the Brutal ordered everyone to be rounded up. I had no idea if Livia had been killed until I saw her chained against a wooden pole. I could see that she had been taken advantage of from her appearance. I remember us making eye contact for a brief moment before Lutisius spoke.

He commanded her to reveal the identity of anyone else who had infiltrated the compound, even offering to spare her life if she did. Yet, she remained silent. I cried uncontrollably as she continued to deny anyone else's presence, even after being whipped. He retrieved his sword and asked her again to reveal the identity of the other intruders."

Vespasian, tears forming in his eyes, said, "With a smile, she affirmed she was the only one. He then stabbed her through the chest. I was devastated. The only reason I managed to survive was my desire for revenge.

My friends and I spent the next several months deciphering the book. The teachings we learned allowed us to manipulate energy. Mortus and I, particularly, became adept at these techniques.

We decided it was time to escape. Mortus and I led a revolt against the guards. The uprising was fierce, and by its end, around 300 guards lay dead.

Our final confrontation was with Lutisius the Brutal himself. We captured him and let the very people he oppressed decide his fate. He met a grisly end, impaled on the wall of his own compound alongside the remainder of his men.

With freedom in our grasp, we commandeered shuttles and returned to Kuiper Station. When I got back, I found out my father had died in an alley after gambling away the last of his money.

Our group, now known as Praetoria, became a beacon of hope for the people of Kuiper Station. We eradicated the corrupt gangs and mercenaries, ensuring no one would ever be taken against their will again."

Ireneus replied, "I understand your suffering, but pain is never an excuse to inflict more pain."

Vespasian responded, "The suffering I inflict is justice."

Ireneus countered, "To me, it appears to be revenge."

Vespasian sighed, "I was hoping we would come to an understanding, but I see now, that is impossible."

Vespasian then extended his hand, freezing Ireneus in place, as Mortus and Silvius drew their swords.

Ireneus struggled to put his hands together, activating Sophus Mode.

Back on Earth, Faunus lay on his bed, reminiscing over playing Ludus Latrunculi with his uncle.

Faunus and his uncle were on the back porch, while Aurora made dinner.

Faunus asked, "Why can I never win, Uncle?"

Uncle Ireneus laughed, "I've just been playing for a very long time."

Faunus joked, "I'd say more like an eternity,"

They both laughed and continued their game.

Uncle Ireneus asked, "Why do you keep asking me to play, knowing I'll win?"

Faunus replied, "One day, I'll beat you but that'll only happen if we keep playing,"

"We're a lot alike," Uncle Ireneus said. "I believe that as long as I work towards peace, it will eventually come."

"Dinner's ready," said Aurora.

Faunus asked, "Mom, can we eat out here?"

Uncle Ireneus gave Aurora a playful smile and said, "Faunus might actually beat me this time."

Aurora laughed. "Alright, we can eat outside."

The game of Ludus Latrunculi between Faunus and Ireneus continued until the sun began to set.

"We should probably head inside soon," suggested Ireneus.

Faunus insisted, "No, not yet. I haven't beaten you."

Ireneus then promptly won the game.

Faunus asked, "Were you stalling on purpose this whole time?"

Ireneus admitted, "Maybe a bit towards the end." He added, "I just enjoy spending time with you."

Faunus looked up at his ceiling as these words echoed through his head. He then sensed a familiar presence. He immediately sat up and put his hands together.

Suddenly, he began to glow. He then said, "Uncle."

Back on Kuiper Station, Uncle Ireneus said, "Faunus."

Silvius, sensing Faunus' presence, said, "The child of prophecy calls out to him."

Vespasian unleashed his lightning at Ireneus, who absorbed it and redirected it back at him. Mortus then channeled lightning into his sword and swung at Ireneus. Ireneus, reacting quickly, blasted him into a wall before he could make contact. Silvius then materialized a spear from the Pompeanus Dimension and threw it at Ireneus, who froze it in midair. Silvius then transported himself behind Ireneus and kicked his leg, causing him to fall to the ground. Vespasian extended his hand, blasting Ireneus into a wall.

Vespasian, breathing heavily, said, "We need to prepare for his arrival."

Back on Earth, Faunus leapt from his bed and shouted, "Uncle Ireneus is alive!"

He ran downstairs and exclaimed, "Mom, Uncle Ireneus is alive!

However, he soon realized that she was not alone. Several Cohort 13 agents were standing in the doorway talking to her.

Aurora turned to him and said, "Go upstairs, I'll handle this."

One of the agents, seeing Faunus, asked, "Is that him?"

Another agent replied, "Yes, that's Faunus Virelius, nephew of Ireneus Virelius and son of Decimus Virelius."

The agent then used his transmitter to inform the other agents that Faunus had been found.

Upon hearing this, Faunus extended his hand and blasted the agent out into the street. Immediately, several other agents, wielding energy weapons, entered the room.

Faunus quickly materialized an ax from the Pompeanus Dimension and channeled lightning into it before slamming it on the ground, releasing a blast of lightning at the agents, causing them to fall to the ground.

Faunus then transported his mom to the Pompeanus Dimension using his Transoculo.

One of the agents threw a smoke grenade while another threw a flash bomb. One of them shouted, "Charge in while his senses are overwhelmed."

Three of the agents charged at Faunus, who leapt into the air and released a Repulsion, sending them flying. He then created a Lightning Ball in his hand and slammed it into the floor, creating a massive shockwave, destroying the house in the process.

Once the dust settled, Faunus transported his mom out of the Pompeanus Dimension.

Aurora, astonished, asked, "Faunus, what happened to the house?"

Faunus laughed and said, "I may have destroyed it, but I did take care of the agents."

Aurora smacked him on the head and shouted, "Where are we supposed to live!"

Faunus, rubbing his head, suggested, "We could stay with Aelia's parents."

Faunus and his mom then walked over to Aelia's house.

Meanwhile, Constantine arrived at the Roman Palace to meet with the President. As he walked down the hallway, he noticed the walls, crafted from pristine white marble, etched with intricate carvings of historic Roman figures. Sunlight poured in through the windows lining the path, casting a warm glow on Constantine's face. The floor, a checkerboard of white marble and black quartz squares, reflected the light.

Constantine approached a colossal door at the end of the hallway, standing several meters high, its olive wood frame inlaid with gold. Two Praetorian Guards, wearing red capes, golden armor, and helmets adorned with red plumes, stood on each side.

The doors then opened, revealing an opulent office. The room was spacious, the floor covered with a plush carpet emblazoned with the emblem of the Roman Republic. Statues of former presidents stood around the room.

Across from the entrance, behind a desk, sat the president. He was surrounded by a massive window that offered a panoramic view of the gardens behind the palace. He wore a red tunic complemented by a purple toga. His fingers were adorned with golden rings, and he had curly black hair with a golden leaf crown on his head.

Constantine said, "President Gaius, it's good to see you again."

Gaius stood up and said, "You mean Gaius Aurelius Titus."

Gaius then laughed as he shook Constantine's hand.

Constantine replied, "You got me."

Gaius said, "Constantine, I heard about the attack on Sardinia and the death of Grand Admiral Tarquinius. The Roman Republic will not take kindly to these losses. The Yuan Empire must be dealt with!"

Constantine grinned, "I've already set a plan in motion."

Gaius asked, "What's your plan?"

Constantine continued, "We'll use the Orbital Defense Satellites to strike military bases across the Yuan Empire. The resulting confusion will allow us to cross the border from Nicea into their territory."

Gaius asked, "It's a good plan, but won't they detect our satellites?"

Constantine replied, "Yes, ordinarily they would, but Cohort 13 will launch a cyber attack to prevent that from happening."

Gaius responded, "Excellent, I'll entrust you with this operation," as a servant poured him more wine.

He then cleared his throat and asked, "You wouldn't know anything about Vincentius' disappearance, would you?"

Constantine replied, "I had no idea. I promise I'll look into it."

Gaius continued, "It's convenient that your brother, Crassus, is next in line after the disappearance of the former Cohort 13 Director."

"Former?" Constantine asked.

Gaius answered, "Yes, I've decided to grant your brother the position. However, I'm deeply disturbed by the reports I've heard. You must not forget that you're the Vice President, Constantine."

Constantine smiled, "Of course, I wouldn't dream of overstepping my authority. I must be going soon; I have another meeting later today."

Constantine stood up and turned towards the door. Before leaving, he looked at the Praetorian Guards as they nodded back at him.

Meanwhile, Faunus and Aurora arrived at Aelia's house.

Aelia smiled and asked, "I haven't seen you in a while. Were you hiding from me?"

Faunus laughed, "I guess I didn't hide well enough since I'm here."

Aelia hugged him tightly. "I was so scared you died in the attack." Pulling back slightly, she asked, "I heard your dad's message. Were you involved in that?"

Faunus replied, "I was. It's a long story." He then wondered, "Where could he be?"

Faunus ran inside and shouted, "Mom!"

Auroria replied, "We're in here."

Faunus quickly ran into the kitchen.

Aurora asked, "Faunus, did you say thank you to Mrs. Pompilius for letting us stay here?"

Faunus turned to her and said, "Thank you."

Mrs. Pompilius smiled, "Don't think anything of it, Faunus. Aelia is really excited that you're here. If there's anything you need, just let me know."

Faunus asked his mom, "Where did Dad go? He should've met up with us by now."

Aurora sighed, "He's probably out drinking."

Faunus said, "I know he's not always reliable, but he should've contacted me."

Aurora reassured him, "Faunus, I'm sure he's alright. He's been through worse."

Faunus said, "I finally learned that my uncle is alive, but now my dad is missing."

Aelia reassured him, "We'll find him, Faunus."

That night, Aelia found Faunus sitting on the windowsill of his room, looking up at the stars. She asked, "Faunus, are you alright?"

He looked at her and said, "I know where my uncle is. He's on a distant space station. I sensed Silvius there too."

Aelia, sitting down beside him, said, "We'll save him, Faunus."

He looked at her as the moonlight shone in her eyes. The same light reflected off Faunus' Transoculo, causing it to appear even brighter. "Your eye is even more beautiful than before," she said.

Faunus gently brushed a strand of hair from her face. "Your's are pretty too." Faunus and Aelia then kissed.

The next morning, Faunus awoke to Aelia landing on top of him. Faunus, startled, said, "Aelia, you're up early."

Aelia responded, "I had to wake you up; someone is at the door."

Faunus sat up and asked, "Who is it?"

Aelia replied, "I don't know, but they mentioned your uncle."

Faunus leapt out of bed and quickly ran downstairs. He then saw a Bishop standing in the doorway talking to his mom.

The Bishop, a middle-aged man with gray hair, wore a red vestment with a black sash and a red cap on his head.

Faunus asked him, "Do you know where my uncle is?"

He replied, "So you must be Faunus. It's a pleasure to meet you. My name is Cardinal Antius. As for your uncle, we have much to discuss."

Faunus asked, "How do you know my uncle?"

Cardinal Antius answered, "Your uncle and I are part of an organization called Collegium. Our organization comprises people from all nations working together toward our common goal. In recent years, we've focused our efforts to restore democracy in the Roman Republic. In fact, it was your uncle who encouraged us to take a more active approach."

Faunus, shocked, said, "This must be how my uncle knew about the Pompeani Cultural Center."

Cardinal Antius replied, "Exactly." He added, "Since you awakened the Transoculo, our ranks will become even stronger."

Faunus replied, "Your ranks?"

Antius replied, "Yes, you've been offered to join Collegium."

Faunus responded, "I'll gladly join your organization once we rescue my uncle"

Antius smiled and said, "That's why I'm here."

He turned to Aelia and said, "You're welcome to join as well."

Aelia replied, "If Faunus is in, so am I."

Cardinal Antius suggested, "You both should come with me to the Vatican."

Faunus shouted, "Let's do it!"

Later on, they arrived at the Vatican. As they approached the entrance, several priests greeted them.

"Welcome to the Vatican," one of them said. "It's an honor to have you here."

Aelia nodded and replied, "Thank you, Father."

Faunus, looking up at the dome, exclaimed, "This place is awesome!"

Cardinal Antius said, "Let me show you around."

Cardinal Antius then led them down a hallway.

Aelia whispered to him, "This place is beautiful."

Faunus replied, "It's like we're in a museum."

Cardinal Antius, overhearing their conversation, smiled. "Indeed, the Vatican has a vast collection of art. I'm glad you like it."

They then arrived in his office. Faunus, looking around, noticed the gold and white marble floor, reflecting the light from the chandeliers above. As he looked up, he saw murals depicting scenes of creation. He then turned to see an olive wood desk surrounded by red marble pillars.

They then took their seats as Lutisius the Berserk, Felix, and several other Collegium members entered.

Faunus stood up and said, "It's good to see you all again."

Berserk responded, "Likewise."

Felix said, "We need to discuss the whereabouts of your uncle."

Faunus replied, "I believe he's being held on a space station."

"How did you know that?" asked Felix.

Faunus answered, "I sensed his presence in deep space."

Berserk remarked, "Your powers have grown stronger. I see that you awakened the Transoculo, very impressive."

Felix elaborated, "Your uncle is being held on Kuiper Station in Lord Vespasian's compound. Unfortunately, the entire station is believed to be under his control, making it unlikely to get in unnoticed. Therefore, we plan to send an elite team that will dock at a port several levels below. From there, the team will move through the ventilation shafts to infiltrate the compound. Beyond this point, we lack schematics, meaning the team will be entering blind. However, Faunus should be able to guide them from there. Once Ireneus is found, the shuttle will land outside the compound. Do you have any questions, Faunus?"

Faunus replied, "I don't have any questions, but I do have a request. I want to bring Aelia and two of my friends."

Aelia smiled and said, "You're really bringing those two?"

He responded, "Of course."

Berserk interrupted, "This is a serious mission; you can't just bring your friends. They'll be a liability."

Faunus replied, "No, they won't, since we're the only ones going."

Berserk, outraged, asked, "Who do you think you are?"

Berserk swung his sword, but Faunus activated Sophus Mode, blocking his attack. The room glowed white as wind swirled around him.

Cardinal Antius intervened, "Enough! Faunus has made his point."

The energy around Faunus dissipated as he deactivated Sophus Mode.

Antius said, "Come, Faunus, I have something to give you." He followed him into the courtyard. They then boarded a shuttle and soon landed outside the Knights of Rome's Castle.

Faunus asked, "Won't the shuttle be detected?"

Antius replied, "No, the shuttle is a modified Lambda Shuttle, so no one will be alerted."

They climbed the steps leading into the Castle and entered the atrium.

Faunus, seeing Mark Anthony's sword, asked, "Is that the gift?"

Antius carefully picked up the sword and said, "As the heir to the legacy of the Knights of Rome, this sword rightfully belongs to you. Take this sword, Faunus, Knight of Rome."

Faunus unsheathed the Spatha. The sword's blade had a blue metallic hue, a crossguard, and a white leather handle.

Faunus, channeling lightning into the blade, said, "I'm ready."

Later on, in Caralis, they met up with Marcus and Lucius.

Lucius said, "The thought of leaving home to go on a dangerous mission is a lot to take in."

Marcus said, "Imagine the stories we can tell."

Aelia said in a serious tone, "This mission means everything to Faunus. He's already turned down additional help. We need to support him."

Lucius conceded. "Okay, I'm with you."

Faunus replied, "I really appreciate all of you. Now, get ready. We'll be leaving soon."

Before leaving, Faunus said goodbye to his mom. "Stay safe," she said, tears forming in her eyes.

Faunus replied, "I'll come back with Ireneus, I promise."

At the spaceport, the group boarded a Collegium shuttle and soon departed Earth. Within a few hours, the shuttle arrived at Kuiper Station, docking discreetly below Lord Vespasian's compound.

Faunus said to the pilot, "If you don't hear from us in two hours, leave the station and inform Collegium that we've been captured."

The pilot responded, "I will, though I hope it doesn't come to that."

Faunus smiled at him before disembarking from the shuttle, concealed in a gray cloak.

Faunus and his friends then entered the ventilation shaft. As they climbed, Marcus began to feel nauseous. "I think I'm going to get sick," he said.

Aelia added, "I feel extremely light."

Lucius explained, "There's no gravity plating in these shafts, which means we're feeling the artificial gravity created by the centripetal force of the station. As we continue to climb, the gravity becomes weaker."

Faunus replied, "You always have the answers, Lucius. I'm glad you're with us."

After a strenuous twenty minute climb, they reached the top. Faunus, looking up, said, "It's like the world is bending upwards."

"That's because we're on a rotating ring," Lucius replied. "The station's structure creates this effect."

Faunus said in a hushed tone, "We're being watched."

Suddenly, two Shadow Guards clad in black armor appeared in front of them.

Faunus stepped forward and said, "Get behind me."

One of the Shadow Guards charged at Faunus with his Spatha. Faunus, reacting quickly, drew his sword to block the attack. The other Shadow Guard extended his hand, blasting Faunus back.

Recovering, Faunus exclaimed, "They can manipulate energy!" He then channeled lightning into his sword and dashed at them. One of them drew his weapon and fired at Faunus, who quickly dodged the incoming shots. He then released a Repulsion, sending them flying.

One of the Shadow Guards, recovering quickly, extended his hand, freezing Faunus in place. Aelia threw a Pugio at him, but he froze it in midair before sending it back at her, grazing her arm.

Faunus transported himself into the Pompeanus Dimension. Reappearing, he threw a Pugio at one of them as he stabbed the other through the chest. Faunus then reattached his Spatha to his belt as the Shadow Guards fell to the ground.

Marcus exclaimed, "You did it!"

Faunus turned to Aelia and asked, "Are you alright?"

Aelia replied, "I'm okay."

He put his hand over her arm and channeled energy into it. "Uncle Ireneus taught me this, but he's a lot better at healing than I am," he said.

Aelia kissed him on the cheek and said, "Thank you."

Later on, they arrived at Lord Vespasian's compound.

Faunus sighed, "There's too many of them."

Marcus whispered, "This won't be easy, but I have a plan. You'll need to transport eight Pugios into the Pompeanus Dimension and materialize one beside each Shadow Guard to take them out."

Marcus retrieved eight Pugios, placing them before Faunus. Faunus then transported them into the Pompeanus Dimension, concealing his presence as he approached the compound. In a swift motion, he dashed past the Shadow Guards, materializing a Pugio beside each one. With a wave of his hand, the Pugios shot toward them.

They then entered the compound. Faunus, looking around, noticed four Pompeani, each possessing either the Spectoculo or the Potestoculo.

Marcus, concerned, said, "We need to find your uncle."

Suddenly, they heard a voice. "I had a feeling you'd come. I sensed you calling out to him."

Silvius then stepped out of the shadows. He wore a white tunic and a brown belt with a Gladius and Spatha attached. He had brown hair, and in his right eye he possessed the Spectoculo, and in his left, the Transoculo.

"These must be your friends," Silvius said, his hand resting on the hilt of his Spatha.

Without hesitation, Faunus dashed at him, but Silvius extended his hand, freezing him in place. Faunus, undeterred, threw a Pugio at Silvius, who transported it into the Pompeanus Dimension.

Faunus then unleashed his lightning. Silvius, reacting quickly, leapt back, releasing his hold over him. Silvius intensified the lightning around his sword, creating plasma. Faunus leapt back just as Silvius stabbed his sword into the ground, releasing a shockwave of plasma.

Silvius, channeling lightning throughout his body, charged at Faunus and kicked him. Faunus quickly regained his footing and taunted, "Is that it?"

Silvius replied, "I have more powerful abilities." He thought, "If I use them, then he'll be able to copy them."

Silvius then unleashed a repulsion, creating a massive shockwave that tore through the atrium, causing the ceiling to collapse. Faunus, reacting quickly, froze the debris in midair, saving the four Pompeani.

Silvius, impressed, said, "You truly are a Knight." He then blasted Faunus with lightning, causing him to release the debris, crushing the Pompeani.

"You couldn't save them, just like you couldn't save your father," Silvius taunted.

"What do you mean by that? Did you..." Faunus said in disbelief.

Silvius replied, "Yes, I killed your father, and soon, you'll meet the same fate."

Faunus, shocked, stumbled back as Silvius' laughter echoed through the atrium. Suddenly, energy began to swirl around Faunus, his body glowing white. In an instant, he appeared next to Silvius, who sidestepped his attack. Faunus then kicked him, sending him flying through a wall.

Silvius, recovering quickly, put his hands together and said, "Resonance." The surrounding area changed to the Knights of Rome's Castle. Faunus, disoriented, leapt back. The illusion faded as Faunus regained his senses.

"That ability is called Resonance," Silvius said.

Faunus, breathing heavily, said to himself, "I'm still not great at absorbing energy," as his Sophus Mode dissipated.

Silvius then channeled lightning into his sword and dashed at Faunus, who parried his attack..

Silvius said, "Resonance", but this time, Faunus closed his left eye. "My Transoculo can see through your illusions," Faunus said.

Taking advantage of Faunus' blind spot, Silvius appeared to his left, his sword crackling with energy as he prepared to stab him. He was then sent flying by a powerful blast. Faunus turned to see Uncle Ireneus standing with Aelia, Lucius, and Marcus. He said, "Uncle, I'm so glad you're alright."

Ireneus smiled and said, "I'm so thankful to have you as my nephew."

Silvius, enraged, retrieved his Gladius from his belt. The lightning intensified around his blades, forming plasma. He then charged at Ireneus, who created a Lightning Ball in his hand. Silvius dodged the attack by leaping into the air, but Ireneus was ready, unleashing a stream of lightning, causing him to fall to the ground.

They heard a voice. "Silvius, you should have anticipated that."

Ireneus turned and said, "Lord Vespasian, you decided to join us."

Vespasian looked at Faunus and said, "The sword of Mark Anthony and the Transoculo. This should be interesting."

Mortus warned, "If they use Sophus Mode; this could end badly."

Vespasian replied, "We'll combine Resonance with plasma attacks." Mortus unsheathed his sword as Vespasian created a stream of plasma between his hands.

"All of you, get behind me," Ireneus shouted. He said, "Sophus Mode," as wind began to swirl around him. Placing his hands together, he said, "Lightning Dragon." In an instant, a colossal dragon made of lightning appeared.

Vespasian, unfazed, said, "Plasma Cloak," surrounding himself and Mortus in a plasma shield.

Ireneus began to move his hands, controlling the Lightning Dragon. Mortus channeled plasma into his Gladius and charged at Ireneus, who extended his hands, launching Mortus out of the compound.

Faunus suggested, "Let's take him together."

Uncle Ireneus replied, "Let's do it." Ireneus then created a Massive Lightning Ball and handed it to Faunus, who transported it into the Pompeanus Dimension.

Faunus appeared behind him, materializing the Massive Lightning Ball in his hand. Suddenly, it vanished as Silvius appeared between them, breathing heavily.

Faunus swung his sword, but Silvius parried the attack. Vespasian then released a Repulsion, sending everyone flying.

Faunus asked, "Marcus, is the shuttle around?"

Marcus replied, "It'll be here soon,"

Vespasian declared, "You will not escape," as he created a Massive Plasma Ball.

The pilot's voice was then heard over Marcus' transmitter, "I can't find anywhere to land."

Faunus instructed, "Land on the ring above us, we'll meet you there."

Marcus asked, "How are we getting over there?"

Ireneus said, "I hope we don't have to walk."

Faunus smiled as he activated Sophus Mode. He said, "Grab onto me."

Suddenly, they appeared on the other side of the ring. Soon, the shuttle landed, and they quickly boarded before departing Kuiper Station. Faunus hugged his uncle. "Decimus is dead," he said, tears streaming down his face.

Uncle Ireneus replied, "I know, but at least he died for what he believed in. He died as a Knight."

Faunus said, "I'm so glad to have you in my life, all of you. I don't know what I'd do without you."

Ireneus smiled and said, "I'll always be here for you."

Aelia added, "We all will."

Back on Kuiper Station, Silvius stood, looking up at the ring above him. He thought, "I wonder what it's like to have a family."

Vespasian declared, "We'll do whatever it takes to capture Faunus, for his eye is the key to what we seek."

Prologue to Chapter Six

Two years have passed since the Caralis Massacre. Since then, the Roman Republic has driven the Yuan Empire back on all fronts, inflicting devastating losses.

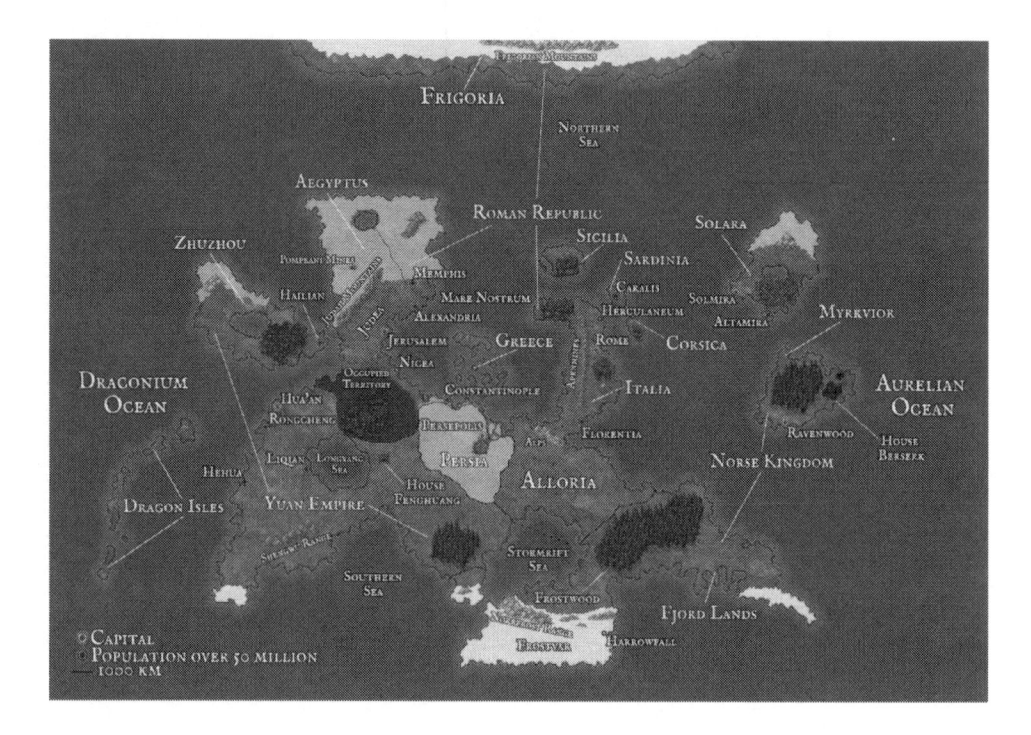

The Roman Republic officially declared Collegium an extremist group and has censored any information about the organization.

Grandmaster Ireneus and Grandmaster Berserk lead the Collegium fleet, which consists of: Pompeani Dreadnoughts, cargo transports, medical frigates, Sigma Shuttles, numerous fighters, and one Omega Cruiser.

Collegium has recently learned of Praetoria's plan to capture more Pompeani possessing the eyes of Eamon. Faunus, now 18 and more skilled than before, has been dispatched to investigate and, if possible, prevent Praetoria from capturing more Pompeani.

Chapter Six

Awakening

Lutisius Station, nestled between two asteroids in the Asteroid Belt, was home to 50,000 Pompeani. The station had several levels and was used as a trading outpost.

As Silvius walked through the station, he noticed a woman with the Spectoculo.

He said to her, "Come with me."

Her husband protested, "No, she's not going anywhere with you."

Mortus, growing impatient, said, "Silvius, you're taking too long. Let's get out of here already."

Silvius, with a scoff, drew his sword and slew the woman's husband. She cried out in anguish as Silvius dragged her back to the hangar.

In the hangar, eight Pompeani, possessing either the Spectoculo or the Potestoculo, were restrained. Mortus entered, dragging a child with the Potestoculo, and threw him in with the others.

The captured Pompeani pleaded for mercy. Silvius retrieved his sword and channeled lightning into it, silencing them. He then reattached his sword to his belt.

Mortus instructed, "Load them onto the shuttle."

Silvius replied, "You do it."

He then heard footsteps echoing down the hallway as Faunus entered the hangar. He appeared taller, wearing a blue cape over his white tunic. His father's Gladius was attached to his belt and he held Mark Anthony's sword.

Looking at Silvius, he said, "It's been a while."

Silvius replied, "You've gotten more powerful since the last time we met. I didn't sense your presence at all."

Faunus warned, "Silvius, this fight won't be the same as last time. I suggest you let them go."

Silvius laughed, "I know, I'm looking forward to it."

Faunus then transported himself behind the Pompeani as he extended his hand, breaking their restraints. Mortus and the Shadow Guards instantly drew their weapons, but Silvius remained unfazed.

Faunus blasted a hole in the wall behind them and said, "Escape through there."

Silvius appeared next to him and said, "I'm ending this."

Faunus replied, "You can try, Silvius." Silvius, smiling, quickly retrieved his Spatha, attempting to stab Faunus through the back. However, Faunus transported across the room, away from Silvius.

Silvius charged at him, wielding his Spatha. Faunus sidestepped his attack, throwing a Pugio at him as he passed. Silvius, reacting quickly, transported it into the Pompeanus Dimension.

They turned to face off, their swords clashing in a shower of sparks. Silvius materialized a Pugio and launched it at him. Faunus, retrieving his own Pugio, blocked the attack. The Pugios fell to the ground, as the sound of metal echoed throughout the room.

Silvius then appeared above him and threw a spear, grazing his shoulder. Faunus slammed a Lightning Ball into Silvius as he landed behind him, sending him flying into a wall.

Faunus then appeared in front of him and kicked him through the wall. He dashed at him, wielding Mark Anthony's sword. Silvius then appeared behind him and threw a smoke bomb, concealing his presence.

Silvius channeled lightning into his sword and stabbed the ground, collapsing the floor. As Faunus fell, he extended his hand, pulling Silvius down with him.

Reengaging, Silvius dashed at Faunus, who quickly transported himself into the Pompeanus Dimension. Reappearing, he released a Repulsion, sending Silvius flying. Faunus said, "Sophus Mode," as his wounds began to heal.

Silvius, undeterred, said, "Resonance." Faunus quickly closed his left eye to avoid the illusion. Silvius then unleashed a stream of lightning at him, but he remained unfazed.

Silvius said, "This is nothing like last time," as he retrieved his Gladius.

Faunus, reattaching his Spatha to his belt, put his hands together and said, "Lightning Beast Raging Lion." As the Lightning Lion charged at Silvius, he extended his hand, absorbing the attack.

Faunus asked, "Had enough yet?"

Silvius laughed and said, "I'm just getting started," as he released a Plasma Repulsion. Faunus extended his hands, absorbing the attack. He then created a Massive Lightning Ball and launched it at Silvius.

The room glowed white as the shockwave tore through the station. As the dust settled, they lay on opposite sides of the room. Faunus then heard an explosion as the hangar filled with smoke. He tried to stand but stumbled, collapsing onto the ground before passing out.

Later, Faunus awoke in a cell aboard Lord Chao's spaceship.

As he looked around the cell, he noticed rusted bars enclosing him and Silvius. A dim light overhead casted a warm glow, reflecting off the metallic walls. He then noticed an ankle monitor strapped to Silvius' leg. Glancing down, he realized he wore one too.

Lord Chao stepped forward and said, "I see you're both awake. Welcome aboard my ship, the *Crimson Dragon*. You've probably noticed the ankle monitors. In the event the signal is lost, either from transporting into the Pompeanus Dimension or tampering with the devices, they'll explode. I can also activate them remotely. Allow me to demonstrate," as he pressed a button.

Faunus and Silvius crumpled to the ground, writhing in pain. "That was level three, but I can increase the intensity if the need arises," he said.

Silvius sat up and said, "He failed to mention the security cameras, so don't try anything."

Faunus asked, "You think I'd do something stupid?"

Silvius replied, "You lack discipline.'"

Faunus angrily replied, "I do not!"

Silvius said, "Whether you would have tried to escape or not, we aren't going anywhere."

Faunus asked, "What does he want with us?"

Silvius answered, "Praetoria eliminated Nexus, and as a former member, he's concerned that he may be next."

Faunus, annoyed, said, "I'm not with Praetoria."

Silvius responded, "Lord Chao won't believe that."

Faunus asked, "Where are our swords?"

Silvius replied, "He took them. I don't know where they are."

Faunus said, "He better not break my dad's Gladius."

Silvius said in a low voice, "It wasn't my decision to end your father's life. He fought valiantly and died as a Knight."

Faunus smiled and asked, "What were his last words?"

Silvius looked up and said, "My son shall surpass the both of us."

Faunus smiled as tears began to form in his eyes. "Thank you, Silvius."

Silvius, astonished, replied, "You shouldn't thank me. I killed your father, and I tried to kill you and your friends."

Faunus replied, "I heard about Vespasian's past. He lived an extremely difficult and painful life. He became overwhelmed by his emotions and was consumed by hatred. You don't have to…"

Silvius interrupted, "You don't know anything about me. You have a family and friends. I have no one!"

Faunus replied, "We can lead the world toward a better future, together. You are far more than just an assassin. You possess the Transoculo, the eye originally possessed by Eamon Pompeanus. You may not have not a family but…"

Silvius interrupted again, "Shut up! You wouldn't understand what it's like to be alone and to be called a failure by everyone around you."

Faunus responded, "You're not a failure, Silvius. You're stronger than me."

Silvius smiled and said, "Perhaps, under different circumstances, we could have been friends."

Faunus turned to him and said, "We still can be."

One of the guards shouted, "Keep it down!"

Silvius said, "I have a plan. I'm going to use Resonance. I need you to create a distraction."

Faunus wondered, "How do I create a distraction?

He then put his hands together as energy began to swirl around him.

Silvius asked, "What are you doing?"

Faunus released a Repulsion, blasting a hole in the cell bars.

Silvius, reacting quickly, released a stream of lightning at Faunus as he channeled lightning throughout his body, deactivating the ankle monitors.

One of the guards said, "They escaped!"

Lord Chao tried to activate the ankle monitors but was kicked into a wall.

Silvius, standing over him, said, "You won't have to worry about Praetoria anymore," as he channeled lightning into his hand.

Lord Chao laughed and said, "Ciao boys," escaping through a hatch in the floor.

They then picked up their swords as an alert sounded.

Faunus smiled and said, "The Collegium Fleet." Delta Fighters then began to fire at the *Crimson Dragon*.

Faunus asked, "Are you coming?"

Silvius replied, "I can't go with you." He smiled, "Thank you, Faunus," before blasting him into a wall.

Marcus soon arrived with Collegium troops.

He walked over to Faunus and asked, "What happened? Are you alright?"

Faunus sat up and asked, "Where's Silvius? Did he escape?"

Marcus replied, "A few fighters managed to escape. I'm glad you had the tracking device on you, or we wouldn't have been able to find you."

Berserk entered and said, "We've secured the entire ship."

Marcus replied, "Very good, let's return to the *Redeemer*."

Once aboard the Omega Cruiser, Faunus was greeted by Aelia in the hangar.

Aelia ran into his arms and said, "I missed you."

Faunus responded, "I missed you too. It's only been a few weeks since I last saw you but it feels longer."

Aelia asked, "Did you find them?"

Faunus answered, "I did."

Aelia said, "How many were captured this time?"

Faunus replied, "Praetoria captured nine Pompeani in total. I saved them, but that doesn't mean they won't come for them in the future. I also fought against Silvius."

Aelia, surprised, asked, "You fought him?"

Faunus responded, "Yes, but then we actually got along, or at least I thought we did."

Aelia asked, "You got along? And why were you on Lord Chao's ship?"

Marcus walked over and said, "Faunus, we need to debrief you about your mission."

Faunus replied, "I'll be right there."

Faunus turned to her and asked, "Is my uncle around?"

Aelia replied, "He left for our base in Yuan near the front lines two weeks ago. However, he hasn't been able to get in contact with the Roman Army."

Faunus replied, "I'll discuss it with Command." He then kissed her goodbye before departing for the command center.

Once there, he was greeted by Akari, Lutisius the Berserk, Marcus, Senators Acacius and Alexius, and Ireneus.

Ireneus, appearing as a hologram, said, "Faunus, it's good to see you."

Faunus replied, "It's good to see you too, uncle."

Senator Acacius said, "We're all glad to see you, Faunus. Now, tell us about your mission."

Faunus recounted, "I freed nine Pompeani possessing either the Spectoculo or the Potestoculo. I also fought against Silvius and Mortus before being captured by Lord Chao. We were imprisoned on his ship for several hours before we managed to escape."

Senator Acacius interjected, "You were both captured?"

Faunus explained, "Yes, Lord Chao was concerned that Praetoria would kill him since they eliminated Nexus, so he captured us."

Berserk noted, "I wasn't aware that Lord Chao was a member of Nexus. We should capture him to find out more about the organization."

Senator Alexius replied, "We can't capture Lord Chao. We're already stretched too thin."

Ireneus said, "Our main priority is the ceasefire negotiations between the Roman Republic and the Yuan Empire. I haven't been able to reach the Roman side of the border, and the proposal I made to the Yuan Empire has been rejected. Faunus, you'll need to cross the border from Nicea. From there, you'll be able to negotiate with General Julius."

Ireneus continued, "In three days, go to the Roaming Roman Tavern in Nicea. You'll meet up with some of our associates there." Suddenly, the transmission cut out.

An officer announced, "I'm detecting several Omega Cruisers and one Titan Cruiser approaching our position."

The *Crimson Dragon* then exploded after being hit with an energy beam from the Titan Cruiser.

Berserk commanded, "Battle stations."

Another officer reported, "We're being hailed by the Titan Cruiser."

Marcus ordered, "Put them through."

Crassus said, "You must be Faunus. I've been meaning to capture you for some time. I'm surprised someone with your reputation is only 18. I see Senators Acacius and Alexius have joined you, no surprise there; we've been keeping an eye on them for a while."

Faunus replied, "You won't capture me."

Crassus responded, "We shall see," before ending the transmission.

Berserk grumbled, "How did they find us?"

Faunus said, "Silvius probably gave away our position."

They then quickly ran to the hangar.

"It's been a while since I piloted a fighter. Marcus, you might actually get more kills than me this time," said Faunus as he climbed into his fighter.

Marcus smiled and replied, "I always get more."

The fighters powered up and flew out of the hangar. Faunus, speaking through his headset, commanded, "All fighters, this is Commander

Faunus. Follow my lead." Twenty fighters fell in behind him, with Marcus pulling up alongside.

Marcus ordered, "Fighters one through ten, follow me." His squadron broke away, attacking the Titan Cruiser's starboard engines. Meanwhile, Faunus' squadron fired missiles at the energy weapon, disabling it.

Aboard the Titan Cruiser, Crassus commanded, "Inform our pilots to target the lead fighter."

Immediately, several fighters closed in on Faunus. He quickly pulled back on the trust as the enemy fighters flew past him. He then fired at them before reigniting his engines, pulling up alongside a Sigma Shuttle. He put his fighter on autopilot and transported himself into the cockpit. He then knocked out the pilots and landed the shuttle in the Titan Cruiser's hangar.

Meanwhile, several fighters fired missiles at the *Redeemer*, creating an explosion that ripped through the ship.

Berserk commanded, "Intensify the port shields!"

The fighters then targeted the *Redeemer's* engines, disabling them. Alarms blared as the ship switched to auxiliary power.

Berserk ordered, "All fighters, return to the Redeemer."

Faunus activated his transmitter and said, "I'm currently on board the Titan Cruiser."

Berserk commanded, "Return immediately!"

Faunus turned off his transmitter. Suddenly, an energy shield appeared in front of him.

He turned to face two Cohort 13 agents. One of them threw a bola, tripping him. The agent then stepped on his wrist, forcing him to release his grip on the sword. He then kicked the sword away from Faunus as he landed a punch.

Faunus quickly transported himself into the Pompeanus Dimension. Reappearing, he released a stream of lightning at one of them. The agent, protected by his armor, remained unfazed. As they drew their energy weapons, Faunus activated Sophus Mode, releasing a shockwave that sent them flying.

Faunus dashed down the hallway and commandeered a Delta Fighter.

He contacted the *Redeemer*, "This is Commander Faunus. I'm aboard a commandeered Delta Fighter."

A communications officer replied, "Berserk has ordered the evacuation of the *Redeemer*. The fleet is to rendezvous at Demos Base."

Faunus replied, "I'll cover your retreat."

Once the fleet retreated, he activated his Coaxial Drive, disappearing into the emptiness of space.

Crassus, glaring, said, "We'll soon wipe out Collegium and eliminate the Knights of Rome for good."

Chapter Seven

Armistice

Saurus Pompeanus stood on a hill overlooking the city of Nicea. His black cape blew in the wind as his eyes glowed amber. He said, "Soon, Faunus, you'll show him the way. You'll lead him out of darkness and into the light. The time is near for the prophecy to be fulfilled."

Meanwhile, Faunus arrived at the Roaming Roman Tavern, his white cloak bearing the crest of the Pompeanus Clan. The tavern was old, with stone walls and a wooden floor that creaked.

At the back of the tavern, a man with black hair, wearing a gray cloak, sat pondering over a Ludus Latrunculi set.

As Faunus approached, he looked up and introduced himself. "It's good to meet you, Faunus. I'm Herminius, archaeologist and professor at Constantinople University. I'm also a member of Collegium and a friend of Ireneus."

Faunus smiled and replied, "It's nice to meet you too," as he took a seat across from him.

Herminius informed, "We'll be leaving soon. Since Ireneus can't cross over to the Roman side, the task falls to us. These negotiations are crucial to secure a ceasefire between the Roman Republic and the Yuan Empire. It's too risky to take a shuttle, so we'll use a hover transport for the journey."

Two Shadow Guards then stood and walked over to them. Herminius began moving pieces on the board, while Faunus remained unfazed. They then drew their Spathas.

Faunus reacted quickly, retrieving his Gladius and channeling lightning into it before swinging his sword, cutting them down.

Faunus turned to him and said, "Let's go."

They looked outside to see Roman soldiers surrounding the building with armored transports and hover tanks. Suddenly, they heard explosions as the soldiers dove for cover.

Herminius suggested, "Let's escape through the back."

Faunus asked, "Who's attacking?"

"Collegium," Herminius answered.

As they stepped outside, an armored transport pulled up in front of them. Suddenly, masked soldiers in black armor with red markings threw thermal grenades at the transport, causing it to explode.

Cohort 13 agents then fired at them. Faunus retrieved his Spatha and dashed at them but a sniper took them out. The building with the sniper then exploded as Faunus hit the ground, hearing the roar of a Delta Fighter overhead.

Faunus, sensing a disturbing presence, said to Herminius, "Meet me outside the city."

Herminius asked, "Where are you going?"

Faunus ran towards the disturbing presence, activating Sophus Mode to sense their location. He then cornered them in an alley, channeling lightning into his swords.

Faunus asked, "Who are you?"

He replied, "Saurus Pompeanus."

Faunus asked, "Are you with Praetoria?"

Saurus remained silent.

Faunus dashed at him but he sidestepped his attack and said, "Resonance." Faunus then looked up to see the Potestoculo in his eyes.

Suddenly, the area around Faunus changed to a burning village. Faunus put his hands together and said, "Counter Resonance."

Saurus said, "Even with the Transoculo, you won't be able to see through my illusion. The Potestoculo is often believed to have hypnotic abilities due to my Resonance technique. In reality, the eye doesn't possess such power; rather, it reflects the connection of its wielder to the Pompeanus Clan."

Faunus asked, "What do you want?"

Saurus replied, "I want to talk to you. Yes, I'm with Praetoria, but I'm not your enemy. I'm Silvius' brother."

Faunus countered, "Silvius doesn't have a family."

Saurus replied, "He's unaware that I'm his brother."

Faunus became enraged and put his hands together, severing the Resonance Link.

Saurus said to himself, "His powers are strong."

Faunus shouted, "How could you stand by and let your brother be used by Vespasian?"

Saurus replied, "It's more complicated than you could understand. I believe that you'll save Silvius and stop Vespasian."

Saurus continued, "Your eye will guide you on your path, but do not let its power consume you. Otherwise, you'll become prideful, and you'll inevitably fail. I'm giving you something to pass on to Silvius, or, if it comes to it, to use against him."

Faunus asked, "What is it?"

Saurus outstretched his hands over Faunus and said, "The power of Eamon belongs to you." He then disappeared.

Faunus thought, "I wonder what he gave me."

Suddenly, he heard explosions as Delta Fighters flew overhead. Faunus then dashed out of the city and met up with Herminius.

Herminius instructed, "Let's get everything loaded," as they began to load supplies onto the transport.

Herminius turned to Faunus and said, "We almost left without you."

Faunus replied, "I sensed a disturbing presence so I had to check it out. It turned out to be Saurus Pompeanus."

Herminius, terrified, asked, "He's here?"

Faunus responded, "Yes."

Herminius commanded, "We're leaving now. Saurus Pompeanus is nearby. Tatius, Cyrus, and Caius, you're coming with us."

Faunus asked, "What's wrong?"

Herminius replied, "Saurus Pompeanus is one of the strongest Pompeani to ever live. There are rumors that he killed an entire division of Praetorian Guards and sliced an asteroid in half."

Faunus said to himself, "I had no idea he was that strong."

They then departed Nicea.

Herminius suggested, "We should inform Ireneus."

Caius warned, "If we break transmission silence, they'll find us."

Tatius sighed, "If Saurus is after us, there's no hiding."

Faunus said, "He gave me something earlier."

Cyrus laughed, "Let me guess, a tracking device."

Tatius replied, "He won't need a tracking device. He can sense Faunus."

Faunus said, "I concealed my presence so he can't find us."

Tatius responded, "That's not going to work."

Suddenly, they heard a Delta Fighter overhead. Herminius quickly turned the transport, narrowly dodging a missile as it exploded behind them.

Faunus then put his hands together and activated Sophus Mode.

Tatius said, "So that's Sophus Mode."

Energy swirled around Faunus as he created a lightning shield around the transport. "I'm not very good at manipulating energy like this," he admitted.

His Transoculo glowed as an energy sword materialized in his hand. The blade glowed white, as though it were burning with white flames. Faunus quickly leapt into the air and swung his blade at the Delta Fighter, slicing it in half as it crashed into the ground. He then landed back on the transport as the energy sword dematerialized.

Herminius said, "That was the Sword of Sealing, one of the weapons created by Eamon Pompeanus."

Faunus responded, "I didn't even know I had it. It just appeared in my hand."

Later that night, Faunus sat gazing at the stars.

A voice said, "The night sky is beautiful, don't you think?"

Startled, Faunus turned to see Saurus standing behind him.

He stood up and said, "How did you get so close without revealing your presence?"

Saurus smiled, "There's still much for you to learn. Your Transoculo gleams in the moonlight while my eyes reflect the light of the sun. Your eye is more powerful than mine, and yet I'm able to see more than you."

Faunus replied, "I don't understand anything you say."

Saurus responded, "Then let's see if we can change that. It's time for you to awaken your powers."

Saurus walked over to him and extended his hand, launching him off the transport. Faunus leapt up and threw a Pugio at Saurus, who sidestepped the attack.

Saurus sighed, "You haven't realized."

Faunus shouted back, "Realized what!"

Saurus appeared behind him as his surroundings changed to Kuiper Station. He said, "I'm not really here."

Faunus channeled lightning into his Gladius and stabbed him through the chest, but the attack passed through him, leaving him unharmed.

Faunus asked, "Am I going to learn Resonance?"

Saurus replied, "You aren't disciplined enough to learn Resonance. The ability requires immense concentration. It took Silvius years to master."

Faunus smiled and said, "If Silvius can do it, then I can too. I'll use Sophus Mode."

Saurus responded, "Sophus Mode allows you to absorb from your surroundings, but you still need discipline to master Resonance. There are those, like myself, who are adept at using it. However, you're different from me. The abilities you use should complement your strengths."

Faunus asked, "Complement my strengths?"

Saurus answered, "Yes, if you combine your strong sensory abilities with your Transoculo, you'll be able to sense targets from a distance and transport to them."

Saurus channeled lightning into his Gladius and said, "You'll have mastered this technique when you can sense me. You'll be fighting for your life."

Faunus smiled and said, "Let's do this," as he channeled lightning into his swords.

He then dashed at Saurus and stabbed him with his Gladius, but his blade passed through him. Saurus released a repulsion, sending him flying. He channeled lightning into his feet and charged at Faunus, stabbing his sword into his shoulder. Faunus collapsed to the ground, thrashing in pain.

Saurus said, "I can use Resonance to make you experience pain. The pain you're feeling isn't real."

Faunus, gritting his teeth, said, "Sophus Mode."

He then dashed behind him and said, "Lightning Beast Raging Lion," while channeling lightning into the form of a lion.

Saurus smiled, "Impressive technique, but you still haven't sensed me."

Faunus put his hands together in an attempt to sense him.

Saurus said, "Imperfect Sophus Mode," as he outstretched his hands, creating a Massive Plasma Ball. He then launched it at Faunus, who extended his hands, absorbing the attack. Faunus created a portal in front of him, then another next to Saurus, before amassing a lightning ball in his hand.

Faunus said, "This lightning ball combines our energies."

Faunus then sent the lightning ball through the portal as he saw a bright flash of light in the distance.

His Sophus Mode deactivated as he collapsed to the ground.

Saurus reappeared and said, "You've done well. Now go, and negotiate a ceasefire between the Roman Republic and the Yuan Empire."

Faunus smiled and said, "Thank you, Saurus. I won't let you down."

Saurus replied, "I have no doubt."

Faunus awoke everyone and said, "I can get us to where we need to go, but I'll need to gather more energy first."

Cyrus laughed, "Anything is better than the transport."

Tatius replied, "That's for sure."

Faunus said, "Let's go," as he created a portal in front of them. In an instant, they appeared in the Roman campsite.

The Roman soldiers stood up in astonishment.

Herminius said, "We're here to negotiate a ceasefire between the Yuan Empire and the Roman Republic."

Faunus added, "We're here so you can go home."

The lieutenant, recognizing Faunus, replied, "I'll take you to see the General."

Faunus and Herminius were escorted to the command center, a large tent at the heart of the campsite. General Julius sat at his desk, with Praetorian Guards on each side. Below them, the emblem of the Roman Republic was displayed on the floor.

The lieutenant said, "General Julius, allow me to introduce Faunus Virelius and Herminius Horace."

General Julius said, "Take a seat."

Herminius asked, "You know Ireneus, right?"

Julius replied, "Yes, I served alongside General Ireneus in many battles over the years. I used to be good friends with him before he betrayed us."

Faunus responded, "The only traitors to the Roman Republic are those who serve their own interests rather than the interests of the people."

Julius smiled and said, "You have a way with words, Faunus. I would expect nothing less from Ireneus' nephew. I've heard a lot about you. Many refer to you as the last knight. Do you believe you're powerful enough to stop us?"

Faunus replied, "No, but I believe I can change you."

Julius said, "Ireneus was wise to entrust you with this mission."

Herminius asked, "Will you agree to a ceasefire?"

Julius looked at his men. "We're tired of fighting. I'll agree to a ceasefire if the Yuan Empire is willing," he answered.

Faunus replied, "Thank you."

Julius ordered, "Tell the men to stand down."

The Praetorian Guards exchanged a brief nod before aiming their energy weapons at Julius. Faunus, reacting quickly, leapt onto the desk and swung his sword, cutting them down.

Julius raised his hand, signaling to his men to stand down.

Herminius said, "This proves that the Roman Republic will turn on its own generals to keep the fighting going."

Julius said, "Thank you for saving my life."

Faunus leapt off the desk and replied, "I'm glad I was around."

Julius turned to Herminius and said, "You may be right. Let's contact Ireneus and arrange a meeting."

Later on, Faunus, Herminius, and Julius met up with Ireneus and General Caishen of the Yuan Empire.

Ireneus smiled and said, "You did well."

Faunus replied, "Thank you. I learned a lot from this mission."

Ireneus responded, "I'm excited to hear all about it."

Julius and Caishen then signed the agreement for a ceasefire.

Julius said, "This is the first step toward peace."

As the agreement was signed, General Julius and Caishen locked wrists.

Chapter Eight

Son of Pompeani

Silvius, concealed in a dark cloak, arrived in the detention level of Lord Vespasian's compound. He waved his hand, deactivating the security cameras as he walked down the hallway. He then entered a cell and lowered the hood of his cloak, revealing his face.

In the dimly lit room sat Prisca, with her dark blond hair resting on her shoulders. At 19, she was the same age as Silvius. She possessed the Potestoculo and wore a plain, gray uniform.

Prisca looked up and shouted, "Silvius!" rushing over to him. "Where have you been? I missed you?"

Silvius sighed, "We're leaving. Let's go," as he released her restraints.

Prisca asked in disbelief, "Silvius... are you leaving Lord Vespasian?"

Silvius instructed, "Put this on," handing her a dark cloak.

Prisca teased, "Are you trying to sneak me into your room? We could've just stayed in the cell. That's what we did last time."

Silvius, blushing, admitted, "We're leaving Kuiper Station. I've had enough of Vespasian."

Prisca said, "I'm glad you decided to take me with you."

Silvius replied, "I need your sensory abilities for my escape."

Prisca, disappointed, asked, "Is that the only reason you're taking me?"

Silvius turned to her and said, "You're invaluable to me."

Prisca, blushing, replied softly, "Good to know."

They walked out of the detention level, heading toward the hangar.

Valeria, seeing Silvius, asked, "Who's with you?"

Silvius replied, "It's none of your concern."

Valeria blasted the cloak off Prisca.

Prisca shouted, "That wasn't nice."

Valeria sighed, "Silvius, she's meant to stay in the detention level unless Lord Vespasian says otherwise."

Valeria grabbed her wrist and said, "I'm taking you back."

As Valeria turned, Silvius appeared in front of her, holding his Gladius to her neck.

"Let her go," he said.

Valeria released her. Silvius then pinned her hand against the wall as he pressed his Gladius against her neck.

Silvius said, "Resonance," as she fell to the ground.

They then continued walking down the hallway.

Silvius asked, "Is Saurus nearby?"

Prisca replied, "He's always been good at concealing his presence, but I should be able to sense him." She closed her eyes and added, "He's with Mortus right now."

Silvius said, "We'll never make it out of here if we have to fight them both."

Meanwhile, Saurus sat across from Mortus, the candles casting a soft glow on their faces.

Mortus asked, "Did you face Faunus?"

Saurus answered, "I did," pouring himself a glass of wine.

Mortus responded, "No one has ever survived a fight against you, except for Lord Vespasian."

Saurus smiled and replied, "Faunus is a formidable opponent."

Mortus said, "Lord Vespasian wants to keep him alive, but I'd rather kill him."

Saurus replied, "He possesses the Transoculo, so it won't be easy."

Mortus asked, "You respect him?"

Saurus responded, "I respect him as an adversary."

Mortus replied, "Be careful that your respect doesn't turn into sympathy."

Saurus said, "Mortus, without sympathy we'll inevitably lose ourselves."

He then activated Resonance, causing him to fall to the ground. Saurus said to himself, "Today, I'll finally tell Silvius the truth."

As he turned to leave, he knocked the wine glass onto the floor, shattering it. He glanced down at the broken pieces before putting on his cloak and walking down the hallway.

Silvius and Prisca then arrived in the hangar.

Prisca warned, "He's coming our way."

Silvius replied, "Keep sensing."

Meanwhile, Saurus entered Lord Vespasian's throne room. The room had dark stone walls and a marble floor. Candles were scattered throughout, casting a soft, flickering light. Near the back stood a throne, hewn from red marble.

Lord Vespasian said, "Saurus, you returned."

Saurus replied, "I came back yesterday."

Vespasian asked, "Did you face Faunus?"

Saurus responded, "I did."

Vespasian replied, "I take it you weren't able to defeat him."

Saurus looked up at Vespasian and said, "I was unwilling to. Though, I probably would've failed even if I tried."

Vespasian asked, "What do you mean?"

Saurus, glaring, answered, "You'll soon be defeated. I'm finally going to tell Silvius the truth."

Vespasian laughed, "The truth. Saurus, even if you tell him everything, he'll still hate you."

Saurus replied, "He has every right to despise me. Regardless, I'll tell him everything and help him escape."

Vespasian responded, "You're a traitor."

Saurus replied, "No, today I no longer betray myself."

Vespasian stood up and said, "You might have beaten me before your injury, but now you're no match for me."

Saurus retrieved his Gladius and replied, "We shall see."

Vespasian glared at Saurus, his eyes glowing amber. The candles around them began to flicker as the two prepared to faceoff.

Saurus dashed at Vespasian and unleashed lightning at him. Vespasian absorbed the attack and redirected it back at Saurus, who quickly dodged it. Saurus then channeled lightning into his sword and stabbed the throne. Vespasian appeared behind him, having dodged the attack, and blasted him through the throne. Saurus, struggling to stand, activated Resonance as Vespasian charged at him, wielding his Gladius. Saurus sidestepped his attack and swung his sword at him. Vespasian quickly parried his blade and released a Repulsion, sending him flying.

Saurus said, "Imperfect Sophus Mode," as he created a ring of white plasma around himself.

He then concentrated the plasma into a ball and launched it at Vespasian. The room exploded in a bright flash of light.

Vespasian said to himself, "This doesn't feel right." He then activated Counter Resonance, causing the illusion to disappear.

Back in the hangar, Silvius and Prisca confronted Saurus.

Silvius confronted him, "How did you know we'd be here?"

Saurus replied calmly, "I didn't."

Silvius said, "I've already severed your Resonance Link," appearing behind him as he stabbed him through the back.

Saurus, coughing, acknowledged, "You've grown powerful, Silvius." In an instant, he vanished before reappearing behind him, unscathed. Silvius, undeterred, released a Repulsion, sending him flying.

Silvius charged at him, but he sidestepped his attack and blasted him into a wall. Saurus then appeared before Silvius, pinning his hand against the wall as he pressed his Gladius to his neck. "You won't be able to escape unless you defeat me," he said.

Silvius said, "Counter Resonance," as the illusion disappeared.

"My eye can see through your illusions," Silvius declared.

Saurus said, "We don't have much time. Lord Vespasian has severed my Resonance Link, and he'll be here soon. I need to tell you the truth before he arrives."

Suddenly, Silvius' surroundings shifted as he found himself in a Roman village.

"The truth?" asked Silvius.

Saurus replied, "Yes, the truth about your past. This is Herculaneum, the city where you were born."

Silvius looked around, observing Pompeani possessing either the Spectoculo or the Potestoculo.

Saurus smiled and said, "That used to be our house."

Silvius asked, "What do you mean our house?"

Saurus looked at him and confessed, "I'm your older brother, Silvius. This is the home we grew up in. That's our mother, Silvestra, and the baby she's holding… is you."

Silvius, shaking, asked, "How?"

Saurus continued, "The man with the black hair and the Potestoculo is our father, Fabius Pomeanus."

Suddenly, the village began to burn.

Silvius asked, "What's going on?"

Saurus sighed, "This is the day we lost everything."

Silvius watched as Lord Vespasian and Praetoria slew Pompeani.

Saurus explained, "Lord Vespasian never forgave Lutisius the Brutal for enslaving him, so Herculaneum became the target of his vengeance. Our parents fought valiantly to protect everyone but were killed. I remember running back to the house when I was attacked by Praetoria."

Saurus paused, his voice softening. "You were so young, yet you intervened and saved my life. Vespasian decided to spare you and take you as his apprentice. I was given the choice to either swear allegiance to him or die. The thought of escaping crossed my mind, but I couldn't leave you behind. So, I decided to join Praetoria."

Saurus then severed the Resonance Link as the hangar reappeared.

Silvius stared into the distance, recalling a memory from his past. Mortus struck him with a metal pole as he fell to the ground.

"You're weak," Mortus said.

Silvius, gritting his teeth, stood up and swung at him. Mortus parried his attack and disarmed him, striking him in the leg.

Silvius collapsed to the ground, clutching his shattered leg.

Mortus said, "You're pathetic." He turned to a Shadow Guard and commanded, "Take him back to his cell."

Silvius shouted back, "I hate you."

Later, Saurus brought him a tray of bread and soup. "Let me see your leg," he said.

Silvius extended his injured leg. "He broke it," he murmured.

Saurus knelt down beside him as he channeled energy into his leg. "I'm not the best at healing, but you should be alright in a few days," he said.

Silvius shouted, "Don't leave me!"

Saurus stood at the cell door as tears welled up in his eyes. He then stepped out of the cell, closing the door behind him.

Silvius felt tears forming in his eyes as the memory faded. He said, "I remember you took care of me."

Lord Vespasian then arrived in the hangar, followed by Mortus, Maximus, Valeria, Cassius, Diana, Titus, Vulcan, Julio, Horatius, and Justinius.

Lord Vespasian smirked, "So, the brothers have come together, casting aside their grievances, to defeat me."

Saurus turned to Silvius and said, "Silvius, take Prisca and escape on the Lambda Shuttle. I'll hold them off."

Silvius, defiant, replied, "No, we'll face them together."

Saurus gently put his hand on his shoulder and confessed, "I've lied to you for so long. I failed you as your older brother, and I know you may never forgive me, but I'll always love you."

Saurus extended his hand, sending Silvius flying back as he remotely activated a shield, separating Silvius and Prisca from the others. He then threw a Pugio at the control panel, destroying it.

Confronting the others, he said, "Use any technique you wish, nothing will work against me."

Lord Vespasian said, "I'll handle this."

Mortus interjected, "My Lord, allow me to assist you."

Saurus then activated Imperfect Sophus Mode as a ring of white plasma formed around him.

Saurus shouted, "Go Silvius!"

Silvius, reluctant, said, "Let's go."

Saurus smiled, as he said to himself, "Faunus will lead him out of darkness and into the light."

They then departed Kuiper Station.

Saurus created a lightning shield as Vespasian and Mortus dashed at him. They circled around, attacking from each side, as they stabbed him.

Saurus said, "I'm over here," as Vespasian turned to see everyone unconscious around him.

Mortus said, "You should've killed us while you had the chance."

Saurus smiled and said, "Imperfect Sophus Mode," forming a massive lightning ball. He launched it at Mortus, who countered with Vis Sigillum, absorbing the attack. Vespasian released Fulgur Anguis, a massive lightning snake. Saurus retrieved his Gladius and sliced the lightning snake in half.

Vespasian, channeling plasma into his sword, dashed at Saurus. Mortus charged in as well, wielding his Gladius. Saurus, reacting quickly, activated Imperfect Sophus Mode Repulsion, releasing a shockwave of white plasma.

Lord Vespasian absorbed the attack with his hand, but Mortus collapsed to the ground, thrashing in pain.

Saurus activated "Resonance," creating clones of himself. Vespasian activated Counter Resonance as Saurus disappeared. Saurus whispered, "Album Flammea Bestia." A massive lion, formed from white flames, appeared, catching Vespasian by surprise. The hangar exploded in a bright flash of flight.

As the dust settled, Saurus lay on the ground.

Vespasian asked, "Where's the Sword of Sealing?"

Saurus, coughing, replied, "I've already given it to someone else. You will be defeated soon enough."

Vespasian channeled plasma into his sword and declared, "You're the one who's defeated," as he stabbed him through the chest.

Vespasian said, "You were once my rival, but you threw everything away for your brother. How pathetic."

Mortus asked, "Should we go after them?"

Vespasian answered, "No, I know where they're going."

Aboard the Lambda Shuttle, Silvius swore, "I won't let your death be in vain, brother. I swear to destroy Praetoria."

Prisca hugged him and said, "Saurus sacrificed himself so we could escape. We need to honor that sacrifice and move on."

Silvius replied, "This path of vengeance is mine to walk alone."

Prisca responded, "I won't leave you, Silvius."

Silvius shouted, "It's not your responsibility…" but he was interrupted by a kiss. "We'll do this together," she said.

Later, they arrived in Herculaneum, stepping off the shuttle concealed in dark cloaks.

Silvius said, "Vespasian knows we're here. Stay close."

Prisca asked, "Why are we here, then?"

Silvius answered, "To learn the truth."

Silvius, noticing a Cohort 13 agent, pulled her into an alley and said, "We're being watched."

He then transported her to the Pompeanus Dimension and dashed toward the Forum, arriving at an abandoned house. In the center of the courtyard stood a broken statue of Lutisius Pompeanus, partially hidden under the branches of an oak tree. Vines crept up the cobblestone walls and onto the red tile roof.

Silvius then transported her out of the Pompeanus Dimension.

Prisca shouted, "You didn't have to do that!"

Silvius replied, "It was the quickest way to get here."

Prisca, annoyed, asked, "Are you saying I'm slow?"

Silvius sighed, "Let's take a look around."

Silvius placed his hand against the oak tree, feeling the rough bark. He then walked into the atrium, observing the broken pillars. He closed his eyes and heard a voice. "Silvius, we're so proud of you. We love you." Silvius collapsed to the ground as tears welled up in his eyes.

Prisca hugged him and said, "It's alright, Silvius, I'm here."

Later, they returned to the Lambda Shuttle.

"We're going to Rome," Silvius said.

Prisca asked, "What's your plan?"

"I need to learn more about the Knights of Rome," Silvius replied. "After that, I'll find Faunus and kill him."

Prisca, startled, said, "You're planning to kill Faunus?"

Silvius responded, "If I don't, Vespasian will come for him, and Faunus isn't strong enough to resist."

Prisca asked, "Are you sure you can go through with it? You told me about your conversation aboard the Crimson Dragon."

Silvius replied, "I killed his father, and I tried to kill him. We'll never be friends."

Later on, they arrived in Rome.

Silvius said, "I disabled the transponder so they won't know we're here. Let's go."

Meanwhile, Constantine sat in his office looking out into the garden behind the palace. He then received a transmission from Vespasian and ordered the Praetorian Guards to leave the room.

Vespasian, appearing as a hologram, said, "I see you have a new office."

Constantine smiled, "Yes, I've recently been appointed President. Crassus convinced the Senate that Gaius ordered the attack on Sardinia, so he's been imprisoned. Is that why you called?"

Vespasian replied, "No. Silvius escaped from my compound. I need you to find him for me."

Constantine, surprised, asked, "What happened?"

Vespasian responded, "Saurus betrayed me, allowing him to escape with a girl."

Constantine replied, "I'll dispatch Cohort 13," as he ended the transmission. "I want every agent dispatched, now!" he commanded.

Meanwhile, Silvius and Prisca walked down a street near the Forum.

Silvius, looking around, said, "I'd like to live here one day."

Prisca smiled and replied, "I'd like to as well."

Cassius, watching them from a distance, said, "Lightning Ball."

Silvius, sensing his presence, blasted Prisca back. Suddenly, a lightning ball exploded in front of him. As the dust settled, Silvius emerged, his cloak singed. He then unleashed a stream of lightning at Cassius, who narrowly dodged the attack.

Sigma Shuttles landed in front of them as Mortus and Valeria stepped out.

Mortus threatened, "Surrender or die."

Valeria, irritated, replied, "Vespasian wants him alive."

Silvius shouted, "You killed my brother! I'm not going anywhere with you."

Mortus retrieved his Gladius and charged at Silvius, as Valeria dashed at Prisca. Silvius threw his Spatha at Valeria as he parried Mortus' attack with his Gladius. Mortus then slashed him across the face with a Pugio. Silvius, recovering quickly, released a Repulsion, sending them flying.

Valeria threw her spear at Silvius, who sidestepped the attack and unleashed a stream of lightning. He charged at her, wielding his Gladius, but Mortus extended his hand, sending him and Prisca crashing through a window.

Silvius extended his hand, collapsing the wall and causing rubble to block the entrance. He then slammed a lightning ball into the wall behind them as he escaped with Prisca.

Cohort 13 agents quickly surrounded the building as Mortus and Valeria closed in.

Cassius leapt down from a ledge, wielding his Spatha. Silvius retrieved his Gladius, blocking the attack as he held onto Prisca. Cassius then kicked him into a wall as he held a Pugio to Prisca's neck.

Silvius shouted, "I give up," tossing his Gladius in front of him.

Cassius smirked, "Lord Vespasian ordered us to kill her."

Mortus and Valeria then arrived as Cohort 13 agents surrounded him.

Valeria taunted, "You've always been weak."

Silvius extended his hand, causing them to fall to the ground, gasping for air.

Mortus, coughing, said, "Lightning Ball."

Suddenly, the lightning ball exploded in a blinding flash of light as Silvius lay unconscious.

Valeria, aggravated, said, "I'm going to kill her."

A voice commanded, "Let them go."

Cassius asked, "Who are you?"

Ireneus discarded his cloak, revealing himself.

Mortus and Cassius dashed at him as he activated Sophus Mode, creating a Massive Lightning Ball. He then launched it at them, resulting in a shockwave that sent them flying.

Silvius, regaining consciousness, threw a Pugio at him. Ireneus caught it and said, "You're safe now," as he waved his hand, knocking him out.

Chapter Nine
Deliberation

Silvius stood on an asteroid as two comets crossed each other above him. Suddenly, the Pompeani Oracle appeared.

The Oracle spoke, "When two comets cross the sky, two eyes will appear. One eye against the other. The fate of the world rests on the result of their battle. The eyes of old will determine the course of the future."

Silvius' Transoculo awakened as the stars circled above him. Slowly, he became aware of a voice. "Silvius, are you alright?" He then awoke, breathing heavily.

"It's alright, Silvius. You're safe," Prisca reassured him.

Silvius asked, "Where am I?"

Prisca answered, "We're at the Collegium base in Rome."

Faunus walked in and said, "I see you're awake."

Silvius tried to reach for his Gladius but curled over in pain.

Prisca advised, "You should take it easy."

Silvius laughed, "I take it you're not here for a fight."

Faunus smiled, "I wasn't planning on it, but if you are, we could."

Aelia said, "Faunus, you should be nicer to him."

Faunus said, "I wasn't..." but was interrupted by Aelia, "I'm glad you're feeling better, Silvius. Let me know if there's anything you need."

Prisca, annoyed, replied, "He doesn't need anything from you. I'm taking care of him."

Aelia responded, "I'm only offering."

Prisca shouted, "Don't be such a bitch!"

Aelia, aggravated, asked, "What did you call me?"

Faunus interjected, "We should let Silvius rest."

Prisca, ignoring Faunus, said, "You may think you're pretty because of your Spectoculo, but that's all you have going for you."

Aelia slapped her across the face and said, "I don't know how Silvius puts up with you."

Prisca tackled her and shouted, "Faunus is too good looking for you!"

Faunus turned to Silvius and asked, "So, how have you been?"

Silvius responded, "I've been better."

Uncle Ireneus walked in and said, "This is no way for ladies to behave."

They both stood up and apologized to each other.

Ireneus smiled and said, "That's better."

Silvius said, "Thank you for saving us."

Ireneus replied, "I'm glad you're alright. I'd like to ask you some questions about Praetoria."

Silvius asked, "What would you like to know?"

Meanwhile, Vespasian, Mortus, and Crassus met with Constantine in his office.

Crassus said, "I've dispatched more agents, but we still haven't found them."

Mortus interjected, "I would've captured him if Ireneus hadn't interfered."

Constantine said, "Faunus and Silvius pose a significant threat to our plans. Capturing them may no longer be an option."

Vespasian, standing near the back of the room, replied, "I need one of them for my research."

Constantine responded, "That's no longer possible."

Mortus replied, "Lord Vespasian isn't asking."

Crassus shouted, "Vespasian isn't in charge here, and neither are you!"

Mortus retrieved his Gladius and channeled lightning into it. The Praetorian Guards immediately aimed their energy weapons at him.

Vespasian commanded, "Mortus, lower your sword."

Mortus lowered his Gladius.

Vespasian suggested, "The Pompeani Oracle prophesied that one of them would die. We may only have to capture one of them."

Crassus replied sarcastically, "How fascinating."

Constantine said, "Vespasian, out of respect for you and your research, I'm willing to go along with this. If one of them doesn't die, though, I'll have no choice but to order their elimination."

Vespasian responded, "We're in agreement then."

Meanwhile, Silvius met with Collegium Command.

Herminius, appearing as a hologram, said, "It's nice to meet you, Silvius."

Lutisius the Berserk asked, "How have the negotiations been going?"

Herminius answered, "Both sides have agreed to a ceasefire."

Senator Acacius replied, "That's excellent!"

Marcus said, "Constantine intends to continue the war, so we must overthrow the government to secure peace."

Silvius laughed. "Cohort 13 has half a million agents, while you only have a few thousand. You'll never be able to overthrow the government."

Marcus replied, "We won't be alone. A few Roman legions have already joined us."

Lutisius the Berserk added, "House Berserk is with you as well."

Silvius said, "You'll still be outmatched."

Ireneus smiled and said, "Our strength comes from each other, not from the weapons we bear."

Senator Acacius asked Silvius, "Are you ready to share what you know about Praetoria?"

Silvius answered, "I am."

Elsewhere, Aelia and Prisca walked through the compound. The area was lush with trees and vibrant flowers.

Prisca sighed, breaking the silence. "I'm sorry about earlier."

"Me too," Aelia replied.

Prisca continued, "I haven't really interacted with people in a while. I'm not the best at getting along with others."

Aelia smiled, "You won't have any issues getting to know me."

Prisca smiled and said, "Thank you. Your eyes are a lot prettier than mine."

"That's not true at all!" Aelia exclaimed. "I always wanted the Potestoculo."

Prisca laughed, "My eyes don't have any abilities."

Aelia replied, "The Potestoculo may not have unique abilities, but it's believed to reflect a strong connection to the Pompeanus Clan. There's a reason the eye is so rare. If you ask me, your eye is way cooler!

Prisca asked, "How do you know that?"

"Faunus," Aelia answered.

Prisca said, "I'm sure Silvius knows a lot too, but he hasn't told me very much."

Aelia asked, "How long were you with Praetoria?"

Prisca replied, "I was never with Praetoria. I was their captive, used for research."

Aelia, disturbed, asked, "What kind of research?"

"Biological," Prisca explained. "Vespasian conducted experiments to learn about the Pompeani eyes."

"That's terrible," Aelia said. "You're safe here."

Prisca smiled back at her as they continued walking through the compound.

Meanwhile, Faunus sat looking out into the courtyard.

Silvius approached and asked, "How's the view?"

Faunus replied, "Better than staring at sand all day."

"I take it you're referring to your mission," Silvius said.

Faunus responded, "I met your brother, Saurus. He gave me something to pass on to you."

"What is it?" Silvius asked.

"The Sword of Sealing. Apparently, it once belonged to Eamon Pompeanus," Faunus replied.

Silvius asked, "How did Saurus get his hands on it?"

Faunus admitted, "I'm not sure."

"Do you know how to use it?" Silvius pressed.

Faunus turned away. "I'm still figuring that out."

"You don't trust me with it, do you?" Silvius said.

Faunus sighed, "It's extremely powerful."

Silvius smirked, "If you managed to figure it out, I shouldn't have any trouble."

Faunus replied, "I'm not an idiot, you know."

Silvius smiled, "We still haven't had our final duel. I'd rather use it against you when the time comes."

Faunus said, "I don't want to fight you, Silvius."

Silvius shouted back, "Praetoria will not relent until you're caught, which is why I must kill you."

Faunus said, "You won't be able to kill me, Silvius, because I won't fight you. The only way we can protect ourselves is if we stand together."

Silvius replied, "You're naive, Faunus. You won't be able to protect yourself for long."

Later that night, Silvius contacted Cohort 13. "I have the location of Collegium's compound," he said. "My only condition is that Faunus Virelius be allowed to escape."

The Cohort 13 agent responded, "We'll ensure he escapes unharmed. Transmit your coordinates."

Silvius confirmed, "I've sent them."

The agent replied, "Understood. We'll be there within an hour," as he ended the transmission.

Silvius woke Prisca and said, "We have to leave."

Prisca, startled, asked, "Why? What's going on?"

"Cohort 13 will be here soon. We can't stay," Silvius explained.

"How do you know that?" she asked.

"I gave them our location," Silvius confessed.

Prisca asked, "After everything Ireneus and Faunus have done for you, you'd betray them?"

Silvius replied, "I have to face Faunus."

Prisca suggested, "We should face Praetoria together."

Silvius said in a serious tone, "I won't risk Faunus being taken. He has to die."

Prisca insisted, "There has to be another way."

Silvius said, "Let's go."

Prisca replied, "No, I'm staying. I may not get along with others, but I won't betray them."

Silvius said, "That's your decision," as he activated Resonance, putting her to sleep.

Ireneus and Herminius watched as Silvius departed the compound.

Herminius asked, "Should we evacuate?"

Ireneus replied, "We're out of time," as troops began to surround the compound.

"I'll talk with them," Ireneus said, walking forward.

A Lambda Shuttle landed as General Cato and Commander Flavius stepped out.

Ireneus asked, "Soldiers, are you going to shoot me? What about you, Cato? We fought side by side during the Persian Campaign. And you, Flavius? We served together at Cohort 13."

Cato replied, "Ireneus, you're under arrest for treason."

Ireneus shouted, "Constantine controls the Senate. He made his brother, Crassus, the Director of Cohort 13. Will you stand by as Rome falls to tyranny, or will you aid me in restoring our Republic?"

Flavius replied, "I'm with you, General."

Cato, hesitant, glanced at the soldiers and said, "I'm with you, too."

They shouted, "Long live the Republic."

In a nearby building, a Cohort 13 sniper reported, "Sir, we've lost control of the situation. Commander Flavius and General Cato are traitors."

Crassus ordered, "Withdraw the remaining agents. We'll deal with those traitors later."

The next day, Faunus watched a transmission from Silvius in the Command Center.

Silvius instructed, "Meet me on the island of Corsica within three days. If you don't, I'll destroy Collegium myself."

"You shouldn't face him alone," Herminius advised.

Aelia said, "I agree."

Ireneus interjected, "Faunus and Silvius will face each other, it's been prophesied. The victor will determine the fate of this world. Faunus, I know you'll do what is right."

Faunus replied, "Thank you, Uncle."

He kissed Aelia and said, "I love you."

"I love you too," she replied, tears forming in her eyes.

Prisca pleaded, "Faunus, please bring Silvius back to me."

Faunus reassured her, "I'll bring him back."

Later, he arrived on Corsica, once home to the Pompeanus Clan. Landing his shuttle atop a mountain, he observed lush forests and rugged mountains. Stepping out, he approached Silvius, who stood on the edge of a cliff, gazing out at the sea. The waves crashed against the rocks below as the wind blew.

Faunus, wearing a blue cloak over his white tunic, stood across from Silvius.

"Corsica was once home to the Pompeanus Clan; now, it lies in ruin," Silvius said, turning to face him.

"This fight won't be the same as last time," Faunus replied.

Silvius laughed, "I've heard that before."

Faunus pleaded, "We don't have to do this, Silvius."

Silvius insisted, "Yes, we do."

Faunus sighed, "So be it."

Silvius drew his Gladius, channeling plasma into it as Faunus retrieved Mark Antony's sword. They then dashed at each other, their swords clashing in a shower of sparks.

Chapter Ten

The Prophecy Fulfilled

Silvius parried Faunus' attack as he released a Repulsion, launching him back. Faunus retaliated by creating a massive lightning ball, but Silvius kicked him, causing the lightning ball to explode. Silvius dashed at him, wielding his Gladius, but Faunus sidestepped his attack, unleashing lightning at him.

Silvius transported himself into the Pompeanus Dimension as Faunus pursued. Silvius released another Repulsion, creating a shockwave of lightning. Faunus leapt into the air, dodging the attack, but Silvius charged, slashing him with a Pugio.

Faunus transported himself out of the Pompeanus Dimension and materialized a spear. As Silvius reappeared, he threw the spear, gashing his shoulder.

He then channeled lightning into Mark Anthony's sword as Silvius launched a plasma ball at him. The plasma ball exploded, destroying Mark Anthony's sword.

Faunus, glaring, retrieved Decimus' Gladius and charged at Silvius. He reacted quickly, releasing Fulgur Anguis, a massive electric snake. Faunus swung his Gladius, destroying the snake in a bright flash of light. He then extended his hand, launching Silvius off the mountain.

Silvius quickly transported himself into the Pompeanus Dimension before hitting the ground. Reappearing, he launched a spear at Faunus, gashing his arm. Faunus leapt down and dashed at him.

They locked blades as the ground cracked beneath them. Faunus created a lightning ball as Silvius countered with a plasma ball. As their attacks slammed into each other, they were sent flying.

Silvius, breathing heavily, activated Resonance, as Faunus closed his left eye.

Silvius, taking advantage of this, retrieved a Pugio and appeared next to him. Faunus, anticipating this, created a lightning ball in his left hand. Silvius, caught off guard, tried to dodge the attack, but Faunus slammed the lightning ball into him, launching him back.

Suddenly, Silvius appeared behind him with lightning coursing through his hand. He then swung at him, launching him off the cliff.

Faunus, reacting quickly, transported himself into the Pompeanus Dimension. As the dust settled, Faunus reappeared with the Sword of Sealing.

Silvius leapt down and said, "You're finally getting serious."

Faunus, activating Sophus Mode, replied, "This ends now." He said, "Lightning Beast Hydra," creating a massive three headed lightning beast.

Silvius countered, "Plasma Beast Raging Wolf," forming a plasma wolf.

The lightning hydra and the plasma wolf charged at each other, resulting in a massive explosion.

Silvius then dashed at him, wielding a Pugio, but Faunus turned and kicked him, sending him crashing through the trees. He then appeared behind him with a massive lightning ball. Silvius reacted quickly, absorbing the attack with Vis Sigillum.

Silvius, exhausted, created a plasma shield, but Faunus appeared next to him with the Sword of Sealing. Silvius quickly escaped to the Pompeanus Dimension, dodging the attack.

Faunus pursued him, but Silvius transported himself out of the Pompeanus Dimension. As Faunus reappeared, Silvius kicked his leg, releasing a blast of lightning that caused him to fall to the ground, writhing in pain.

Faunus then swung the Sword of Sealing, cutting off Silvius' left arm and gashing him across the eye.

Silvius screamed in agony as he looked up at Faunus.

Faunus said, "It's over, Silvius."

Silvius, gritting his teeth, said, "Resonance."

Faunus activated Counter Resonance, causing the illusion to disappear. He then collapsed to the ground as the Sword of Sealing disappeared.

Silvius pleaded, "Kill me."

Faunus shouted, "Shut up! I'm not going to kill you. I've proven that I can protect myself, so there's no reason for us to fight."

Silvius acknowledged, "You've always been stronger than me. I let my fear take over, and I betrayed you and your friends. I'm sorry."

Faunus said, "I've shown you there's another way."

Silvius laughed, "I suppose you have."

Faunus smiled, "Saurus believed in you. He gave me the Sword of Sealing to pass on to you."

Silvius asked, "Now that we've finished our fight, can I have it?"

Faunus replied, "As long as you don't use it against me."

They laughed as they looked out at the horizon.

Meanwhile, Crassus, Senator Remus, Admiral Leonidas, General Octavian, and Captain Aulus met with Constantine in his office.

Constantine said, "We need to discuss the situation immediately."

Senator Remus shouted, "The Roman Republic is on the brink of civil war!"

Admiral Leonidas asked, "How many legions remain loyal to us?"

General Octavian responded, "Five legions."

"This is outrageous!" Senator Remus exclaimed.

Captain Aulus added, "That's less than half of our forces."

Crassus interjected, "Cohort 13 has already begun to eliminate the traitors. Once they're dealt with, we'll appoint new generals to command the legions."

Admiral Leonidas countered, "Replacing the generals won't be enough. The troops are rallying behind Ireneus."

"If we kill Ireneus along with the other rebel leaders…" General Octavian began, but Crassus interrupted.

"Killing Ireneus would only make him a martyr," Crassus said.

Constantine asked, "What about Collegium? How many fleets do they have?"

Captain Aulus replied, "Five fleets."

Admiral Leonidas sighed. "We're significantly outnumbered."

Constantine said, "We still have to deal with Faunus and Silvius."

Crassus added, "Our intelligence indicates they engaged in combat, but we don't know the outcome."

Constantine suggested, "Let's ask Lord Vespasian."

Lord Vespasian, appearing as a hologram, said, "If you're asking about Faunus and Silvius, I don't know."

Crassus, annoyed, said, "You're supposed to be handling them."

Vespasian replied, "I will. In due time."

Constantine said, "We're outnumbered, Vespasian. We need your help."

Vespasian smiled, "You've backed yourselves into a corner, haven't you?"

Admiral Leonidas asked, "How do we prevent a civil war?"

"The future of the Roman Republic is uncertain," he said. "I'll send Mortus, Cassius, and Valeria to assist you."

He then ended the transmission.

Crassus complained, "We look weak."

Constantine replied, "We are weak. Now, let's prepare for the coming battle."

The following day, Ireneus gathered Collegium at a campsite five kilometers from Rome.

Ireneus said, "Romans, lend me your ears. We've come here today, united in our cause to restore the Roman Republic. We fight for our families, for the men beside us, and for our freedom." He added, "Marcus will brief us on the attack."

Marcus locked wrists with Ireneus and said, "Thank you."

"Good morning," Marcus began. "Today, we retake our Republic. The attack has three components: The siege of Rome, led by myself, General Ireneus, and Commander Felix. The attack on the surrounding military bases, led by General Julius and General Cato. Finally, the space battle, led by General Berserk, Commander Lucius, and Admiral Iccius. General Herminius shall oversee the Command Center. While we currently outnumber the enemy, don't let yourselves become complacent."

He shouted, "Today, we shall be victorious."

"Long live the Republic!" they shouted back.

Meanwhile, Cohort 13 agents stormed the Collegium compound in Rome. One agent fired a rocket launcher at the entrance as they entered the compound. A Lambda Shuttle landed in the courtyard as Crassus stepped out.

"Sir, the compound has been abandoned," an agent reported.

Crassus commanded, "Evacuate the men, and order our bombers to destroy the compound."

Outside the city, General Ireneus marched with 300,000 men as Delta Fighters roared overhead.

Marcus, riding alongside Ireneus, suggested, "Once we enter the city, I recommend having one tank accompany each division."

Ireneus agreed as he relayed the order.

He then announced, "We're about to enter the city."

Suddenly, Delta Fighters and Gamma Bombers roared overhead.

Marcus shouted, "Everyone take cover!"

Collegium fighters intercepted the bombers as Cohort 13 fired on their shuttles.

Ireneus shouted, "Take cover," as a shuttle crashed in front of them, sending a cloud of smoke into the air.

Felix said to Ireneus, "General Cato reported in, their legions have sustained heavy casualties."

Ireneus commanded, "Begin the attack on Cohort 13 Headquarters."

Meanwhile, General Berserk and Commander Lucius commanded the fleet.

Berserk instructed, "We have to keep their cruisers occupied. Delta squadron, engage the Omega Cruisers, attack pattern Epsilon. Gamma squadron, engage the Titan Cruiser and disable its weapon. Beta squadron, attack Cohort 13 Headquarters. All remaining fighters, protect the fleet."

Beta squadron began their attack, launching missiles and firing energy projectiles at Cohort 13 headquarters. Cohort 13 retaliated by firing missiles from turrets positioned around the compound. One of the Gamma Bombers was hit, causing it to crash into the compound, resulting in an explosion.

Meanwhile, Constantine sat in his office as Cohort 13 agents reported in.

An agent informed, "Sir, Cohort 13 is under attack."

Another agent reported, "Sir, we lost two Omega Cruisers."

Constantine commanded, "Order the Titan Cruiser to fire on their command ship."

Another agent reported, "Sir, Praetoria has arrived."

Constantine replied, "Send them in."

Mortus, Cassius and Valeria then entered.

Mortus advised, "You'll lose unless you turn Collegium against the people."

Constantine asked, "What do you suggest?"

Mortus replied, "Order the Titan Cruiser to fire on Rome."

Constantine, shocked, responded, "That'll endanger our troops."

Cassius said, "Then Collegium has already won."

Constantine sighed, "Have the Titan Cruiser fire on Rome."

Captain Aulus, aboard the Titan Cruiser, received the order.

Admiral Leonidas, overhearing, said, "No, we're not firing on Rome."

Captain Aulus insisted, "We have orders."

Admiral Leonidas replied, "We're not firing on our own civilians."

A Cohort 13 agent shot him. He turned to Captain Aulus and said, "Captain Aulus, you're in command now."

Captain Aulus ordered, "Charge the energy cannon and prepare to fire on Rome."

An officer reported, "The energy cannon is fully charged, sir."

Captain Aulus commanded, "Fire."

In the Forum, Ireneus and Marcus watched as the energy beam exploded in a blinding flash of light. The shockwave rippled outward, collapsing skyscrapers and decimating the surrounding area. Constantine watched from his office as Rome began to burn.

An agent reported, "Sir, our communications have been disabled."

Another agent informed, "Sir, we have reports of power outages throughout the city."

Constantine, furious, shouted, "That hurt us more than them."

Mortus replied, "A necessary loss."

Back in the Forum, Ireneus shielded Marcus and Felix from the debris.

Ireneus commanded, "I want a casualty report."

Felix said, "A few tanks survived, but we've sustained heavy losses."

Marcus, horrified, said, "All these people died because of us."

Ireneus reassured him, "We're not responsible. This was a cowardly move to turn the people against us."

Aboard the Quasar, Lutisius the Berserk ordered, "Divert all power to the forward shields. Prepare to attack the Titan Cruiser."

Lucius added, "All remaining bombers disable the weapon."

The Pompeanus Dreadnaught fired on the Titan Cruiser as Gamma Bombers disabled its weapon.

Aboard the Titan Cruiser, an officer reported, "We lost the weapon."

Captain Aulus commanded, "Launch fighters, and prepare to engage the Pompeanus Dreadnuaght."

Lucius said, "We won't last long against that cruiser."

Berserk commanded, "Lucius, order the evacuation. I'm going to destroy the Titan Cruiser."

The officers turned to Lutisius the Berserk and said, "We're staying, sir."

Berserk commanded, "Deactivate the shields, and divert all power to the engines."

Lucius evacuated aboard a Lambda Shuttle with the remaining men as the Quasar flew toward the Titan Cruiser.

Aboard the Titan Cruiser an officer reported, "Sir, the Quasar is on a collision course."

Captain Aulus shouted, "Take evasive action."

Berserk shouted, "For Pompeani," as the Quasar slammed into the Titan Cruiser, creating a massive fireball.

Meanwhile, Collegium troops disembarked from Lambda Shuttles as Cerberus tanks fired at Cohort 13 Headquarters. The headquarters was an imposing structure composed of three interconnected octagons, each linked by passages. At the center of the innermost octagon was a landing area with several Lambda Shuttles. The building, made from concrete, stood two stories tall. Below ground, several levels were interconnected by underground passages, and a high speed train system connected the headquarters to various locations throughout Rome.

Crassus said, "We need reinforcements."

An agent reported, "Sir, Collegium troops have entered the compound."

Crassus shouted in anger, "Evacuate Cohort 13 to our base in the Alps, and prepare my shuttle."

The next day, Ireneus and his troops arrived at the compound.

Ireneus said, "We did it Decimus. We've finally taken Cohort 13 Headquarters."

Marcus suggested, "We should use this compound as our base of operations."

Ireneus replied, "I agree."

Felix reported, "I've spoken with Lucius, the remaining cruisers have surrendered."

Marcus, relieved, said, "The battle is almost over."

Ireneus said, "Not yet, we still have to secure the Senate and the Roman Palace."

Meanwhile, a Lambda Shuttle approached the Roman Palace. A Cohort 13 agent reported to Constantine, "Sir, a Lambda Shuttle is approaching at high speed."

Constantine instructed, "Raise the shield."

Faunus and Silvius leapt from the shuttle as it crashed into the gardens behind the palace.

Mortus said, "I sense a disturbing presence," as he turned towards the window.

Silvius dashed toward Constantine's office, wielding the Sword of Sealing. He leapt up and crashed through the window, landing in Constantine's office.

Silvius swung the Sword of Sealing at him, but Mortus parried his attack. He then quickly disengaged as the Praetorian Guards fired at him.

Constantine smiled, "I see you were victorious."

Silvius said, "Faunus better get here soon to save you from me," as he channeled lightning throughout his body.

Mortus channeled plasma into his Gladius and charged at Silvius, who released a Repulsion, sending him and the Praetorian Guards flying. Silvius leapt onto his desk as he swung the Sword of Sealing. Mortus extended his hand, launching Silvius into a wall.

The Praetorian Guards escorted Constantine out of his office as they turned to face off.

Outside the palace, Faunus fought Cassius and Valeria. Cassius created a plasma ball and launched it at Faunus, who sidestepped the attack. Valeria then channeled lightning into her spear and threw it at him. Faunus released a Repulsion, launching her into a wall. Cassius drew his Spatha and swung at him. Faunus reacted quickly, activating Sophus Mode and kicking his sword out of his hand.

Faunus then turned to see Mortus charging at him.

Silvius shouted, "Faunus, look out!"

Faunus was kicked into a wall as Mortus, Cassius, and Valeria ran off.

Faunus stood up and said, "I wasn't expecting that."

Silvius sighed, "Constantine escaped."

Faunus replied, "We'll deal with him later."

Silvius responded, "No, I'll deal with him. I have to atone for my sins."

Faunus laughed, "You're always so dramatic."

Silvius replied, "I'll meet up with you later."

Faunus said, "You better come back."

Silvius smiled, "I will," as he locked wrists with him.

Faunus said to himself, "We'll have Rome under our control by the time you get back."

Chapter Eleven

Atonement

Hidden in the snow covered peaks of the Alps, was a Cohort 13 compound. The stronghold had numerous hangars, an intricate tunnel system, and fortified turrets. Crassus, Senator Remus, Senator Servius, and General Octavian met with Constantine in the tower.

Constantine said, "We're here to discuss Project Ventriloquist, the solution to our current situation."

"I've never heard of Project Ventriloquist," said Senator Remus.

Crassus replied, "It remained classified."

"Yes, until now," Constantine said. "The project uses genetic material from Knights to create clones with their abilities. We implant microchips to ensure their obedience. Lord Vespasian has contributed to our research over the years."

Senator Servius, unsettled, asked, "How many died because of this research?"

"It required many subjects, but the results have been worth it," Constantine assured.

General Octavian asked, "Where are these clones kept?"

"In cryogenic stasis, on the research level of this facility," Crassus answered.

Meanwhile, Silvius approached the compound. A squad of Roman Centurions, wearing white armor and red capes, armed with energy rifles, stood guard.

A Centurion reported, "I'm detecting a target."

"Move to intercept," another Centurion ordered.

Silvius' cloak billowed in the wind as snowflakes swirled around him. He transported himself in front of them, wielding the Sword of Sealing. He then channeled lightning into the blade and stabbed the ground, creating a shockwave of lightning.

Silvius looked up at the compound, his Transoculo glowing as he appeared in one of the hangars. He released a Repulsion, destroying the Sigma Shuttles, and sending a shockwave through the compound.

"What was that?" Crassus asked.

An agent reported, "Sir, there was an explosion in one of the hangars."

Another agent reported, "Sir, we lost contact with a squad."

Constantine ordered, "Lock down the facility and secure the research level."

Senator Remus and General Octavian stood up.

Constantine reassured them, "Take your seats. We're safe here."

Cohort 13 agents and Centurions entered the room as metal blast shields lowered over the windows.

Silvius continued down the hallway. Roman Centurions surrounded him, cutting off his escape.

Silvius, unfazed, released a plasma Repulsion, creating a shockwave of plasma that lit them on fire.

A Centurion communicated, "Lock down the corridor," as energy shields were erected.

Silvius slammed him into a wall, knocking him out.

"We trapped him," Crassus reported.

"Neutralize him with the knockout gas," Constantine ordered.

Silvius activated Resonance, making it appear as if he had been knocked out.

"Sir, he disappeared," one of the Centurions reported.

Silvius then transported himself out of the Pompeanus Dimension and killed the remaining Centurions.

Crassus said, "He's approaching the Command Center."

"Sir, we identified the intruder as Silvius Pompeanus," an agent reported.

"Get me Lord Vespasian," Constantine commanded.

Vespasian appeared as a transmission and asked, "Constantine, how goes the war?"

Constantine replied, "Silvius has entered the compound. We need to secure the research level."

Lord Vespasian smiled and said, "Destroy the facility; I have no interest in the research."

Crassus shouted, "Your apprentice infiltrated our facility. This is your responsibility. I'm ordering you to…"

Vespasian interrupted him. "You've already been defeated," he said. "Die well my friend," as he ended the transmission.

Constantine's face turned pale. "Vespasian betrayed us."

Crassus ordered, "Evacuate the compound, and initiate the self-destruct sequence."

Senator Remus asked, "What about the research?"

Crassus commanded, "Destroy it. Otherwise, Collegium will learn about our plan."

Silvius unleashed his lightning, melting the door as he stepped into the room. The Praetorian Guards, Centurions, and Cohort 13 agents immediately aimed their energy weapons at him.

Silvius said, "It's over Constantine."

Crassus deactivated the blast shields covering the windows as light poured in.

A Lambda Shuttle then fired into the room, killing the Senators and General Octavian.

Silvius quickly transported himself into the Pompeanus Dimension as Constantine and Crassus took cover. They then escaped onto the shuttle as Silvius reappeared.

The Lambda Shuttle then launched missiles into the room. Silvius extended his hands, shielding himself from the explosion.

Silvius then channeled lightning into the Sword of Sealing and threw it at the Lambda Shuttle, causing it to crash. Silvius looked down at the debris and said, "It's finally over."

Suddenly, the facility began to self-destruct, causing the tower to collapse. Silvius quickly leapt off the tower and transported himself into the Pompeanus Dimension before hitting the ground. Reappearing, he observed the destruction.

Silvius said, "I probably should've held back," as he looked at the smoldering debris.

Meanwhile, Praetoria gathered at the Knights of Rome's Castle in Florentia. The castle, situated on a hill, was in ruin. A hole in the ceiling allowed light to enter, bathing Vespasian in its warm glow.

Vespasian opened his eyes and said, "Constantine has been defeated."

Valeria, annoyed, replied, "We'll be branded criminals by the new government.

Maximus laughed, "We've always been criminals."

Cassius replied, "Yes, but now we have to be more cautious."

Valeria said, "Nexus and Pompeani are already hunting us. Soon, the Roman Republic and Collegium will join them."

Vespasian stood up and said, "I'm disbanding Praetoria for now."

Mortus countered, "You can't disband Praetoria without a consensus."

Maximus, tears welling in his eyes, said, "This is my family."

Valeria agreed, "He's right. We're a family."

Vespasian smiled and said, "Mortus, Maximus, Valeria, Cassius, Diana, Titus, Vulcan, Julio, Horatius, Justinius... you are all my family. To protect this family, we must disband. I'll send you out in pairs, so none of you are alone."

Mortus, tears forming in his eyes, asked, "Who will you be with, my Lord?"

Vespasian smiled, "I won't be alone, Mortus. I have all of you. Even if we're apart, we'll remain a family."

As the members of Praetoria departed in pairs, Vespasian remained behind. He looked up at the sky and said, "We'll all be together again soon."

Later, Silvius met up with Ireneus and Faunus at the Knights of Rome's Castle.

Silvius, wearing a white tunic with a blue cape, knelt before them in the atrium. Faunus drew Decimus' Gladius and said, "By the will of the Order, by the will of Rome, rise, Silvius Pompeanus," as he knighted him.

Silvius turned away and said, "I'm unworthy."

Ireneus replied, "Silvius, you're as worthy as any who has come before you."

Faunus smiled and said, "Decimus would want you to have his Gladius."

Silvius, tears streaming down his face, took Decimus' Gladius.

Silvius locked wrists with Faunus and said, "I pledge myself to defend the Knights of Rome."

Ireneus said, "This is a new era."

They then departed for the Senate.

The Senate building, situated near the Forum, had a domed roof and quartz pillars lining its exterior. Marble stairs led up to the entrance. Inside, the Senate chambers were arranged in a semicircle, with wooden seats and marble desks for the Senators. Above, a second level provided seating for the public to watch the proceedings. The Speaker of the Senate presided from behind a large wooden desk, overlooking the room.

Ireneus, Faunus, and Silvius sat down as Herminius greeted them, "It's good to see you. Senator Alexius is about to speak."

Senator Alexius addressed the Senate, his voice echoing through the chamber. "Article IV of the Roman Constitution stipulates that, in the event the government no longer acts in the interest of the people, it is the duty of the people to abolish it and institute a new government."

"Collegium and the Military have acted in the interest of the people to abolish the government. Constantine abused his position to accumulate power and turn the government against the people," Alexius continued. "Constantine is responsible for genocide and prolonging the war with the Yuan Empire. He's also guilty of intimidation and covert surveillance."

"I hereby request the following legislation," he declared. "The immediate dissolution of Cohort 13, the immediate and thorough investigation of all Senators and Praetors, an immediate ceasefire with the Yuan Empire, and a withdrawal of all Roman troops from the region. The release of all political prisoners, the reestablishment of the Knights of Rome, the immediate pardon of all Collegium members and supporters, and finally, an election for all vacant government positions."

"Senators, I implore you to vote for this bill and restore our Republic," Alexius concluded.

Virgile, the Speaker of the Senate, said, "All those in favor of the legislation."

Senator Acacius and the other Senators voted in support of the bill.

Virgile announced, "Senator Alexius' bill has passed."

Faunus turned to Ireneus and said, "We did it, Uncle."

Uncle Ireneus, tears forming in his eyes, replied, "We did it," as he hugged Faunus.

Silvius turned and looked at Prisca. Prisca, noticing him, looked away.

Silvius walked over to her and said, "Prisca, I'm sorry for leaving you. I know I hurt you, and you may never want to see me again…" but before he could finish, Prisca kissed him.

"I love you," she said.

Silvius replied, "I love you too."

A few months later, Collegium gathered at the Roaming Roman Tavern in Nicea.

Silvius and Ireneus sat at a table, playing Ludus Latrunculi.

Silvius exclaimed, "I won!"

Ireneus replied, "I'm impressed. Faunus has never been able to beat me."

Faunus said, "Uncle, don't tell him that."

Silvius offered, "I can teach you how to play, Faunus."

Faunus shouted, "You're always showing off!"

They laughed. Faunus looked at his arm and asked, "How's the new arm?"

Silvius replied, "I'm still adjusting, but the biological replacement has been good."

He turned to Ireneus and said, "I heard you've been appointed Grandmaster."

Ireneus laughed, "There weren't a lot of other candidates."

Faunus locked wrists Herminius and said, "Congratulations on the win."

Herminius replied, "Thank you."

Silvius asked, "You won?"

Herminius said, "Yes, Alexius and I were elected as the President and Vice President of the Roman Republic. Faunus, I heard you'll be the next Grandmaster."

Faunus replied, "One day, but for now, I still have a lot to learn."

Silvius laughed, "That's for sure."

Faunus shouted, "Silvius!"

Aelia, Marcus, and Lucius joined them.

Aelia kissed him and said, "Congratulations, Master Faunus."

Marcus added, "I've been appointed Grandmaster of Collegium. Do I get a kiss?"

Aelia laughed and replied, "Congratulations Marcus."

Lucius added, "Yes, congratulations."

Faunus asked, "Lucius, you've been hired by the University, right?"

Lucius replied, "Yes, I'm now a Professor at Constantinople University."

Aelia said, "That's great!"

Macus added, "Nicely done."

Faunus took Aelia by the hand and said, "We'll be back."

He then led her to a hill overlooking the city. "Aelia, you've been with me from the beginning. I can't imagine a day without you," he said. He revealed a golden ring, got down on one knee, and asked, "Aelia Pompeanus, will you marry me?"

Aelia exclaimed, "Yes!" as she hugged him.

Aelia put on the ring and kissed Faunus as the sun began to set, casting a golden glow over the horizon.

The End

Index

Atrium - A central hall or entrance area.

Gladius - A Roman short sword.

Imperfect Sophus Mode - The technique used by Saurus Pompeanus to concentrate energy into a single point, amplifying the power of his attacks.

Ludus Latrunculi - A Roman board game similar to chess.

Optoculo - This eye appears blue with a white swirl pattern and is the transitional stage to awakening the Transoculo. The eye allows the user to see energy and access the Pompeanus Dimension.

Potestoculo - This eye appears amber and reflects the user's strong connection to the Pompeanus Clan.

Pugio - A Roman dagger.

Repulsion - Creates a shockwave that expands outward.

Resonance - The technique used by Saurus and Silvius to create illusions, allowing the user to share memories or stimulate another's senses.

Sophus Mode - The technique used by Ireneus and Faunus to absorb energy from their surroundings and amplify their own power. It requires discipline and immense concentration to master. The technique remains a challenge for many, as the user must be at peace with themselves.

Spectoculo - This eye appears blue and allows the user to see energy that is normally invisible, enhancing their senses.

Spatha - A Roman longsword.

Transoculo - This eye appears blue with a prominent white swirl pattern and is the final evolution of the Optoculo. The eye allows the user to effortlessly transport objects into and out of the Pompeanus Dimension.

Transportation Technique - The technique used by Faunus and Silvius for instantaneous transportation through portals. These portals are invisible to most but can be seen with the Optoculo or Transoculo. The portals are unstable, lasting only a few seconds, so the user must act quickly to transport through them.

Tablinum - A reception room.

Vis Sigillum - Warps the surrounding space to absorb an attack.

Made in the USA
Columbia, SC
11 February 2025

55e1a494-e686-4f12-91f4-9b8f6bd192b5R02